Suddenly the burning grip of his hands on her shoulders disappeared. The boy let her go. She stayed where she was, out of breath and confused.

Anger bubbled up in him as he stepped back from her. "I'm deaf," he said. He hoped he was yelling. The girl backed up but didn't run; he had her attention. Jake tapped his chest with his thumb, then his ear with his index finger, and brought his open hands together in front of him. *"I'm deaf,"* he signed angrily. He watched her eyes widen in comprehension. "Deaf," he said again, enunciating the *f* so there was no mistake.

Amanda blinked hard. The boy's voice was nasal and muffled, as if he had a bad cold, but the word was painfully clear.

Other Point paperbacks you will enjoy:

point

TELL ME HOW THE WIND SOUNDS

Leslie Davis Guccione

SCHOLASTIC INC.
New York Toronto London Auckland Sydney

ISBN 0-590-41714-2

12 11 10 9 8 7 6 5 4 3 2   2 3 4 5 6 7/9

Printed in the U.S.A.   01

For
Captain Bennett of the Nancy L
and
Andrew,
with love

Acknowledgments

All my characters are fictitious and come entirely from my own imagination, but I'm grateful to those who helped me breathe life into my story with their technical assistance.

Thanks to my editor, Ann Reit, at Scholastic; my agent, Denise Marcil; the Guccione family; Nancy, Skip, and Billy Bennett; Duxbury Harbormaster D.C. Beers, III; and especially Suzanne Stout.

To My Readers

The characters in this story use two languages, spoken English and sign language. When someone speaks, I have used the usual quotes. When someone signs, the dialogue is printed in *italics*. If a character speaks while signing, I have put the italicized words in quotes: *"Look at me, when you speak . . ."*

Jake Hackett uses a combination of Signed English and American Sign Language. What you read in italics is a translation of sign into everyday English, not necessarily a literal translation of each sign. Jake is only as representative of the hearing-impaired world as Amanda is of the hearing.

Chapter 1

Amanda Alden first saw the boy on her third day on the island. As usual, she was sitting on the rocky bluff contemplating her misery, telling herself that her father had absolutely no understanding of what she was missing being away from home. He didn't care at all. It wasn't as if she didn't see him every other week all year long. Joint custody took care of that.

Her father, Dr. Bradford Alden, was a college professor and an authority on Colonial America. He'd been offered the chance to rent Pilgrim House, a cottage on Massachusetts' Clark's Island, the island from which the Pilgrims scouted the shoreline and chose Plymouth as their first settlement. Even Amanda's mother had agreed the education would do her daughter good.

So here Amanda sat, already missing her friends back home in Pennsylvania. At fifteen, Amanda had little interest in exploring her much-talked-about Pilgrim ancestry with her father, stepmother, and two pesty little half brothers. She had even less interest in doing it from some musty old house on a tiny hunk of land so small there were no roads, cars, or telephones.

She had propped herself among the warm rocks that separated the bluff from the pitiful excuse for a beach, a beach that stretched a hundred yards into mud. The air was ripe with the smell of silt and tidal flats. The low tide and lumpy granite only increased her misery.

A figure of a boy emerged from the beach plum bushes and hedge roses as Amanda tuned in the unfamiliar Plymouth and Boston radio stations on her boom box. The boy was well down the beach and, under the bright June sun, hardly more than a silhouette.

Amanda squinted, her boredom leaving her momentarily as she watched him. He was dressed in waders strapped over his bare shoulders, and he held a rake in one hand, a metal mesh basket in the other. Amanda turned off her radio and stared as he continued out onto the flats, leaving small glistening pools in his tracks. She grimaced at the thought of the cold silt full of saltwater creatures as the boy, looking for clams, worked the mud with his rake and bare hands.

"Gross," Amanda whispered. The glare was too bright for her to stare for long, and the rocks were becoming unbearable under her thin bathing suit. With a sigh she shifted and stepped cautiously down onto the pebbled beach, then looked back at the antique Cape Cod-style house on the bluff. If she returned, she'd have to help with the cleaning or, worse, mind the boys, who were only five and seven. Instead, she began an aimless walk south along the beach to the tip of the island.

The clammer was on her left, out in the flats. Amanda looked at the distant sails and at the Plymouth skyline, which made up the horizon, then she walked carefully on, avoiding the barnacled rocks and ribbons of kelp in her path. What houses there were on Clark's Island were deserted, still shuttered against the off season. After half an hour of nothing but gulls and sandpipers for company, Amanda turned around to head home.

As she came around the bend at the beach roses, she stopped in her tracks. The clammer was in her path, bent over his basket. Amanda's heart jumped. He was cute and he wasn't much older than she. Sixteen? Seventeen at the most, she decided as she pressed a fist against the side of her leg. She smiled.

He turned his head quickly as he caught sight of her in his side vision and he stared, surprised that she didn't look familiar. She was of average height, a head shorter than he was, with hair that fell around her face in different shades of blonde. She had on lipstick, and there were tiny gold studs in her ears. With her haircut and pastel bathing suit, she looked sophisticated. His expression remained solemn as he tried to place her. An intruder. She lifted her chin haughtily in response to his gaze and he realized he was being rude.

Amanda felt a rush of wariness that kept her heart racing. She tugged at the leghole of her bathing suit as the breeze snapped her hair against her face. His dark hair was wet; there was a smudge of mud on his chin. She was close enough to see smudges of sunblock on his bare shoulders and that his eyes were as dark as his hair. He was looking at her so intently that her cheeks flushed. Her wariness shifted to confusion. She wanted to get by, back to her towel, closer to the house. He was staring so hard he could have memorized her!

A seagull shrieked and Amanda looked up; he followed her glance. Fear prickled her skin when he still remained silent.

"I'd like to get by," she said, not looking at him. He didn't move.

"Excuse me," Amanda added, this time with force. Relief replaced the fear as he stepped aside. He gave her a tentative nod.

Without looking back, she marched ahead gingerly, still sidestepping the rocks and weeds, her skin raised to gooseflesh. He was still staring. She could feel it. At the rocks, she gathered her things and snapped her radio back on for company. When Amanda finally stole a glance back down the beach, the clammer's spot was empty.

Jake Hackett walked the path and ignored the raspberry canes scratching his waders. He climbed the slope past the summer houses and crossed the flat spine of the island, which opened onto the back acreage of his family's farmstead. By the time he reached the clearing, the turmoil in his chest had settled and it was easier to breathe.

4

He shouldn't have stared so hard or stood in her path so long. The way she had looked on the beach . . . she must have been angry to begin with. He should have made her understand. Her smile had dazzled him, but the memory of the fear on her face was painful. He closed his eyes. Idiot, he thought to himself.

Jake knew every family on the island, many second- and third-generation the way the Hacketts were. On his island there wasn't any struggle to make himself understood or put people at ease. He thrived in the piney isolation and primitive conditions that were no more silent for him than the rest of the world. Away from town, from school, the pressure eased. Sometimes he didn't even think about being deaf.

He reached the back of the house and washed down his clams with the garden hose, then turned it on his waders. When he'd pulled the waders off his jeans, he cupped more of the water and threw it on his face and shoulders, shivering as it trickled down his bare back. The girl was probably staying in the old house the Pilgrim Society owned, the only one likely to be filled with strangers. Jake sighed and threw his waders over the clothesline. He was angry with her for making him feel foolish. She had no right here, on *his* island, making him self-conscious. No right.

He went barefoot into the kitchen and dropped the basket of clams on the counter. His mother was at the sink and she ran one hand smoothly over the other. *Nice*, she signed.

He nodded. "Supper. Tonight."

When Sharon Hackett pointed to the refrigerator,

he shuffled the contents and made room for the clams, then pulled out a peach and a carrot. From the kitchen the view was westerly, to the inner side of the island, Duxbury Bay, and the mainland town of Caterham. Moving through the channel markers from open water was the familiar sight of a thirty-two-foot lobster boat. Jake tapped his thumb and open hand twice on his forehead. *Dad's coming.*

Jake left as abruptly as he'd arrived. He headed for the paddock and watched his chestnut mare as she ambled over. The boy finished the peach and offered the carrot on his open palm to the horse. He climbed over the fencing, and while Lightning chewed, Jake stroked her neck, letting his chest and shoulder absorb the vibrations from her powerful jaws. He moved his hands over her warm hide and let it soothe the ache in him.

When Lightning had finished the carrot, Jake slipped the bridle over her head. He hoisted himself onto the mare's bare back as Stephen Hackett was killing the engine of his boat and securing the *Sharon* to the mooring. Horse and rider came over the field of wildflowers, loped along the beach, and waited. Jake shaded his eyes and watched his father row the dinghy to their pier, but his chest was tight as the image of the Pilgrim Society girl drifted back into his head. The episode had broken the day's rhythm; he couldn't shake it.

When his father had stowed the oars and cleated the dinghy, Jake slid from the horse. It was nearly four o'clock and Stephen Hackett had left the house at three-thirty in the morning. Jake read the fatigue and frustration in his father. Everything inside him tightened more.

Many fishermen thought the Hacketts were crazy to live on the island all summer because it added hours to the grueling daily routine. The base of the commerical lobster operation was in Caterham, across the channel. The Hacketts spent the rest of the year in town. Jake, and his two sisters before him, went to Caterham High School, and his mother taught kindergarten. Caterham was crowded and full of tourists in the summer. The island farm was an anchor, a balm against the rest of the world for more than just Jake.

To cut down on daily trips, Steve Hackett sometimes stored a few days' lobster catch in oversized metal mesh baskets called cars. Like regular traps, their place in the bay was marked by small painted buoys that floated on the surface. Now the boy watched his father clomp down the pier in his heavy knee-high boots.

Jake signed, *Lose more traps?*

His father nodded. "Kids. Nearly a hundred pounds."

Jake circled his heart with his fist. *Sorry.*

They walked the hill with the horse between them and Steve Hackett stooped to yank up a handful of black-eyed Susans. He tapped his chin twice with his thumb. *For Mom.*

At the paddock Jake tapped his father, and with quick, fluid gestures, asked about the following day. His father's confusion made him smile.

"Pay attention," Jake said in his muffled voice.

Steve sighed. "Go easy on your old man."

Jake made it simple: Left hand rose up from under the right, *morning*; both hands scissored index and middle fingers, *lobster*; he touched his fingertips together and moved them forward in a *V, boat*.

His father laughed, pointed at his son, and raised his eyebrows.

Jake nodded.

"Sure, I could use the help," Mr. Hackett said, "and the company."

Jake smiled. A day aboard the *Sharon* meant a day without another chance encounter on the beach. The next day he'd be on the boat until supper. It was the first time Jake had used work as an excuse to avoid the island.

After dinner Amanda volunteered to pick raspberries for breakfast. It gave her reason to escape her half brothers and dish detail. As her stepmother heated water on the stove for the soapstone sink, Amanda grabbed a small pail.

"Take your time and explore," Nancy Alden said, as her stepdaughter pushed open the screen door.

"I'll be home by dark," Amanda replied.

There was at least an hour of daylight left. Without a destination, Amanda followed the deep green paths that sliced across the overgrowth covering most of the island. She had on jeans and a fleece top to protect her arms from the thorny canes. Raspberries grew wild, thick, and tangled with the scrub pines, beneath towering evergreens. As Amanda made her way, she pulled at the ripe fruit gently and popped many of the berries into her mouth while filling the bucket. In twenty minutes she'd made her way into the heart of the island, grateful for her sweatshirt as the temperature lowered with the sun.

Where two paths intersected, Amanda turned left, surprised to find an opening onto a broad, flat meadow. She walked across the field to an out-cropping of rock that rose from the flat ground like a great gray whale. A commemorative inscription was chiseled into the rock and Amanda ran her fingers over it as she read. *On the Sabbath Day Wee Rested. December 20, 1620.*

"Pilgrim Rock," she whispered, a sudden re-minder of why this part of her family was on the island. The air was still around her. She was shel-tered on all sides by the thick woods, yet the sea breeze whistled in the pine tops above her. It was an eerie, eternal moan when the thin trunks swayed. She shivered. Was it the thought of her *Mayflower* ancestors, freezing and alone out here on their way to Plymouth? Or the sudden *caw, caw, caw* above the trees? The fine hair prickled along the back of her neck, and she looked up at the dusky light as a single gull soared in the air current. "I'm being silly," she whispered.

She'd had enough creepy feelings on the beach without letting her imagination run wild in the dying sunlight. Amanda turned away from the inscription. As she tried to remember which path to follow, movement caught her eye, across the meadow at the edge of the woods.

Already tense, a jolt of fear dissolved her common sense. A horse, nearly the color of the tree trunks, stood under low branches. On the animal's back, the boy from the beach sat staring.

Chapter 2

Amanda's glance locked with his. The boy's wide brown eyes bore into her from across the clearing and masked his own surprise. No smile, no greeting. It paralyzed her like a fawn caught in a car's headlight.

She tried to think. She couldn't. She couldn't move. Which path was hers? Which turn had she taken? A pulse pounded in her ears as she imagined the boy charging from the shadows on the horse. She wanted to close her eyes and have him vanish as he had that afternoon. Slowly she turned away from him, found the opening into the woods that was hers, and began to walk back the way she'd come.

Halfway across the meadow, she heard the whinny. It was right behind her, so close she imagined breath on her neck, and her heart jumped to her throat. This time Amanda bolted. The pail fell at her feet as she tore for the path at the far end of the field.

Jake's heart thundered and slammed against his ribs. Part of him wanted to rein in Lightning and turn for the farm, but he needed to explain. The girl didn't understand, and everything he did made it worse. From Lightning's back, he watched her drop the pail. The berries spilled as she began to run. He let her go, hating the feelings she stirred in him. She'd nearly reached the woods when he made the decision. He nudged the mare into a canter with his bare heels and rode past the girl. At her path, he turned Lightning around and slid onto the ground.

Amanda balled her fists and stopped as the boy blocked her way. Her head filled with the scent of the summer grass and the laboring horse.

"Leave me alone! I mean it. Stop following me. Stop staring."

Her fear made her angry, and her blue eyes flashed as she looked from the boy to his horse. "What do you think you're doing?" There was no answer. Instead the boy reached over and took her by the arm.

Amanda pulled back. In the middle of a nowhere island, the horse was the one creature she felt familiar with. She tore the reins from the boy's hand and threw herself onto the mare's back as easily as he had. The boy yelled something she couldn't understand and, as she dug her sneakers into the horse's flanks, she was yanked to the ground, crashing on top of the boy.

Jake took the brunt of the fall and, as he pulled himself onto one knee, the girl punched him. Pain seared his ribs. The blow nearly knocked the breath out of him. The girl scrambled to her feet, deepening his anguish with her terror, and tried to free herself. This time he grabbed her wrist and held on. "Wait."

Amanda yanked her arm, but his grip was like a vice.

"Wait," he tried again.

She didn't hear anything but the pulse pounding in her head. She was too frightened to understand — or care — what he was saying. They stood together, breathing hard, one as angry as the other. Tears blurred her vision as she brushed her free sleeve over her eyes.

Jake let go of her and pressed his hand over the pain in his rib. She didn't run, which was a surprise. When he could breathe, he straightened up and read her angry expression. The girl was swearing at him and rubbing her wrist as she spoke, impossible to understand. A tear slid along the side of her nose. It made him desperate. This time he shook her by the shoulders.

Amanda balled her fists again, but suddenly the burning grip of his hands on her shoulders disappeared. The boy let her go and leaned heavily against a pine tree. She stayed where she was, out of breath and confused.

Anger bubbled up in him as he stepped back to her. "I'm deaf," he said. He hoped he was yelling. The girl backed up but didn't run; he had her attention. Jake tapped his chest with his thumb, then his ear with his index finger, and brought his open hands together in front of him. *I'm deaf*, he signed angrily. He watched her eyes widen in sudden comprehension. "Deaf," he said again, enunciating the *f* so that there was no mistake.

Amanda blinked hard. The boy's voice was nasal and muffled, as if he had a bad cold, but the word was painfully clear.

Jake made a *V* at his eyes and twisted his wrist to her, touched his left fist with his index finger, and tapped his chest. "Look at me," he interpreted. "I can read your lips."

Amanda stared rudely, flushed first from fear and now humiliation. Words wouldn't come. Fury was written all over him.

Jake continued as the girl stared. Let her see what it felt like not to understand! *I didn't hear you on the beach. I didn't try to scare you in the field. You were stupid to run away*, he told her with his gestures. Her expression gave no indication that she'd understood, only that she was horrified to the point of tears. Good!

Deaf! All the anger and indignation Amanda had planned to heap on him melted into a hot ball of embarrassment. She stepped back, unable to think of what to say, how to respond. There was nothing in his expression to frighten her, just sadness and confusion and so much anger. The boy was a mirror of herself. She blushed again, and the color crept up her neck and into her cheeks.

Jake tried to control his ragged breathing, tried to think what to do next. The girl was rubbing her wrist, but as he put his hand out she pulled away. He pressed his sore rib and turned to look for Lightning. He walked to the mare and tethered her to a birch tree. It cleared his brain, gave him time to think, but when he turned back, he found — as Amanda had on the beach — that the spot was deserted.

Amanda ran. She tore down the path, under the thick canopy of summer leaves, through the shadows, and over the island. Who cared what the boy thought? She hated this place and he was just part of it. So what if there'd been a terrible misunderstanding? So what if she'd hurt him? So what? She stumbled, exhausted, onto the wrong path and took the long way, finally arriving at the back of the Pilgrim House in the dark. She could hear the shouts of the little boys as they played at the edge of the bluff, and smell traces of the charcoal grill.

Amanda slumped against a tree. Humiliation burned in her chest; she wasn't ready to face anybody. Again she scrubbed tears away, and as she listened to her stepmother call the boys, Amanda ran once more . . . through the pines at the edge of the lawn, past the clothesline and outhouse.

A derelict family cemetery was separated from the undergrowth by the remains of an iron fence. What headstones there were slanted at crazy angles, more likely from frost heaves and neglect than from vandals. It was too dark to read the epitaphs or the generations of initials carved into the enormous trunk of the beech tree that hung over the fence like a nosy neighbor.

Amanda sat down and expected gooseflesh. The place was creepy enough in the daylight, but she was too full of shame and embarrassment to have room left for fright.

She pulled her knees up and watched the dim gaslight glowing from her kitchen window. The screen door slammed and a beam of light sliced the dusk. Even with modern plumbing, Todd and Eric were going to the outhouse; high adventure.

Amanda rested her forehead on her knees. On her left hand she twisted a large ring made to fit her finger with bands of adhesive tape wound around it. Oh, to be home with Christopher!

Amanda had started dating Christopher King in May, and by the end of school, she was the envy of every girl in her class. The night before she and her family had left for Massachusetts, he'd surprised her with his ring and she'd promised to keep it on until she saw him again. It seemed like forever until the end of the summer.

Now all Amanda wanted was to be home with Chris, at a party with music and laughter and good times. Lockwood, Pennsylvania, was home, a place where the image of the deaf boy's face, as he tried to make her understand him, wouldn't block out everything else.

She stayed in the dark for a long time until her stepmother called her. When Amanda came around to the kitchen, Nancy Alden was at the door. "There you are. I knew you were around somewhere when I found the pail of raspberries on the stoop. Come on in now."

Amanda blanched. The empty pail was sitting next to the sink and a colander full of berries sat under the old-fashioned pump.

* * *

Hours later, still awake, Jake lay in bed and looked out at the night. Sometimes he thought he could remember how the lighthouse sounded, low and froggy, every ten seconds in heavy weather. He looked at the stars. The air from the open window brushed his cheek. The breeze was sweet with the scent of honeysuckle that clung to the shingles. Change was in the air, and he was restless with the pain and the risk of it. The girl, all dazzle and anger, was part of that risk.

Her world was out on the beach, across the channel, out where kids his own age might be partying with music, steaming their stolen lobsters, washing them down with sodas, maybe beers taken from comfortable Caterham houses or bought with fake ID's.

The girl stirred him, the way he stirred up the sea bottom when he kicked at it. Jake massaged his temples against a grinding headache and elbowed his pillow as he waited for sleep. He closed his eyes, but he still saw her recoil from him as he tried to make her understand.

At four A.M., Stephen Hackett started the engine of the *Sharon*. While she gurgled on the mooring, he snapped on the VHF marine radio and the rest of the electronic equipment in the wheelhouse. He had an AM/FM radio rigged with speakers in both corners of the windshield, but when Jake was along, he left it off.

The Hackett livelihood came from a shrinking stretch of unpolluted waters, a pie cut down to its last slice. Life the way Jake lived it depended on a man willing to rise before first light and fight the poachers and the elements, even the draggers who tore up the sea bottom with their chain nets.

From the bow, Jake slipped the line from the chock, dropped the chafe gear into the water, and signaled to his father that the boat was free of the mooring. As the *Sharon* nosed out into the channel, Jake worked his way back over the foredeck. His jump into the cockpit renewed the pain in his rib, and he rubbed it as he moved up next to his father.

"Bellyache this early?"

Jake pretended not to understand.

His father repeated the question.

"You know I can't hear you with the engine running," Jake said carefully. The old family joke earned him an affectionate poke. *Hunger*, he added in sign, grateful that his father dropped the subject and handed him a muffin.

Jake's hearing and speech had been normal until he was six. However, meningitis had left him profoundly deaf. Without the ability to hear himself, his speech changed, too. It was hard to make himself understood, and he knew how muffled and odd he sounded when he spoke. His rare attempts were kept for family and close friends, precisely because of the look strangers, like the girl, gave him when they heard him talk.

After Jake finished his muffins, he pulled on the foul-weather pants that hung in the wheelhouse and watched the lighthouse as the *Sharon* passed beneath it and moved toward open water.

Both Hacketts were just short of six feet. "Big enough to wear your old man's gear," Steve mouthed slowly.

Jake adjusted the shoulder straps and flexed his biceps in a Popeye imitation. The silence between them grew easy. Aboard the boat, the roar of the engine made hearing difficult anyway, and both Hacketts signed in rough shorthand.

Jake balanced himself against the trawl racks and let his body absorb the engine's thunder and steady vibrations. Open buckets of salted bait waited at the stern, and the air was full of the smell of fish heads and flounder spines. Anxious seagulls matched the *Sharon*'s speed as they swooped down over the wake. It was as familiar to him as his horse and his island, and he began to relax.

Once they reached the green-and-white Hackett buoys that marked the traps below the surface, Jake concentrated on hauling up the trawls. There was barely time to think of anything else. The traps were hoisted from the ocean floor with a hydraulic pulley, then set on the rack at the boat's sidedeck. His father removed the catch and banded the claws shut while Jake rebaited the traps. Father and son worked until early afternoon, lost in the task and the labor. Then they nosed the boat toward the mainland. The lobster catch was moderate, but Jake sensed his father's acceptance and it boosted his spirits.

They returned to the channel, and by the time they reached the Hackett pier, Jake had stored the foul-weather pants and rubberized work gloves. As the boat idled, Steve Hackett touched his fingers to his lips. *Thanks*.

Jake smiled and signed, *good day, dinner, don't be late*, then jumped to the pier. He waved his father off and watched the boat head across the channel for the Caterham market. The island was hot com-

18

pared to the open water, and he yanked off his flannel shirt as he walked. The June sun had baked the smell of fishy bait and sea bottom on him.

Lightning grazed in her paddock, the absence of the lawn chair near the house told him his mother was on the sand. There was a distant view of the *Sharon* and her wake. The day's rhythm was undisturbed.

Jake squirted the hose over his bare shoulders, and his muscles quivered under the shock of the cold well water as the sea breeze blew the droplets across his skin. Much of the afternoon was left; Lightning whinnied impatiently.

When she was bridled, he led her from the paddock and rode bareback over the Hackett pasture, which was separated by a low rock wall from the pine woods and their paths. Jake couldn't bring himself to ride the beach; from his farmstead there was no way to tell who might be there. With a nudge, he turned the mare in the opposite direction, but stopped again when they reached the woods and the path to Pilgrim Rock. Lightning shook her mane restlessly, as if losing patience with her master.

A spring began to coil in Jake's chest. Sharply this time he nudged his bare heels against the horse's flank, gripped her wide ribs with his denimed legs, and cantered over the land that was his. The girl, the stranger, had no right to take away his freedom, to make him feel like a prisoner on *his* island. He had half a mind to gallop back to the Pilgrim House again. This time he wouldn't return a berry pail. This time he'd scare her so badly she'd spend the whole summer inside and stay out of his life.

Chapter
3

Amanda nearly turned back half a dozen times. Her head ached and her hands were clammy. As she walked, she rubbed them on her shorts and talked to herself. "Don't be a geek," she whispered more than once. She wasn't afraid, exactly. How could she be? It was daylight, sunny, the end of the afternoon, . . . nothing to be scared of. Except her feelings, she thought glumly.

She crossed the open meadow and this time barely glanced at Pilgrim Rock or the inscription. At the opening of the woods where the boy had sat on his horse, she stopped. She jammed her hands in her pockets and followed the path until she came up to the back of a white clapboard farmhouse. A rake and clamming basket were on the porch. A shirt lay there, too, and waders hung on the clothesline. She'd found him.

"Now what?" she whispered, feeling like a Peeping Tom. There was a whinny from the barn and she turned. Did the boy have a family, someone she could talk to? Were they deaf, too? Why was she doing this? Amanda headed for the barn quickly, before she lost her nerve.

The familiar smell of hay and horse and well-worn leather calmed her down as she stood against the doorjamb and inhaled. However, wafting over it was the pungent aroma of dead fish and traps, far stronger than she'd smelled on the beach. Amanda wrinkled her nose as she made out the shapes of empty bait buckets and wire mesh lobster pots.

Almost dead ahead of her, the boy was in a stall, brushing the mare. His back was to her, and she could see the energy pass from his right arm into the brush and along the horse's flank. He was intent, lost in the task, and she wished she could see his face.

Jake kept brushing, as if he could work the tension out of himself by sweeping the bristles over Lightning. He closed his eyes and sensed the mare's agitation. Somebody was approaching.

He anticipated a tap from his mother, back from the beach, anxious for help with dinner, anxious to get at what was bothering him. She worried too much. They all did.

The skin tingled across his bare shoulder blades. "Not now," he said slowly, with exaggerated clarity. He turned. His heart thundered erratically against

21

his ribs. The girl from the beach was leaning against the stall.

Sunlight beamed halos around her hair. She wet her lips and shifted from one sneakered foot to the other. Jake stood with the brush poised in midair. They waited, stared, and waited.

The girl moved. Jake watched the light play off her shoulders, amazed as she pulled a carrot from her pocket. She made no move to talk. She barely looked at him. Instead she moved between the stall and the horse with her hand open. Lightning bent and took the treat.

The girl's hands were small, and she wore a signet ring bound with adhesive tape on her left ring finger. That must have been what bruised his rib. He touched the tender spot and watched her pat the horse. She scratched the mare's forehead; her lips moved. She was talking to the horse as if she'd known the animal all her life.

Jake felt invisible. She was like some sprite who'd dazzled him and now she was charming the horse, the last part of what was his. How long was she going to stand there looking at Lightning?

She took a step back, then walked past Jake. When she'd gone by, she bent over a bucket, scooped some feed, and carried it to the bin. She smelled fresh, even over the horse and traps, like soap. He felt light-headed, confused.

When Lightning bent to eat, the girl left the stall and disappeared around the partition. He felt stupid as he stood with the grooming brush. He smelled like dead fish, the bay, and the horse. He let a long, painful moment pass in the hope that she'd left the barn. She hadn't. She was leaning against the tack wall, letting hay drift between her fingers. He put the brush on the shelf just by her hair and she flinched.

The boy was caught in a shaft of light from the doorway, angry, staring. Amanda watched him notice every blink, every breath she took. She tried not to feel frightened. She'd concentrated so hard on the trip over the island, through the woods, she hadn't thought about this part. She had no more idea of what she was doing than he did. All she had was a feeling and a need to make things right. The boy turned from her to leave the barn and walked through the light toward the double doors.

"Wait," she cried out.

He kept walking.

She forced herself forward. Though her hand trembled, she touched his shoulder, and he stopped in his tracks. She took a deep breath, put her hand up, and when he looked from her face to her fingers she signed the letter *H*. Next she flipped her wrist and raised her pinky to *I*. *Hi*. She dropped her hand.

Amazement changed his features from guarded to wide open. His brown eyes were never still. The boy looked at her fingers and face. He looked at her until she flushed and laughed.

You sign? You understand sign? he said with his hands.

The girl didn't respond.

He looked at her cautiously.

Amanda cleared her throat. "A girl at school . . . a year behind me . . . in some of my classes . . ." Finally she shrugged her shoulders.

23

Jake smiled and touched the side of her mouth with his fingertips. "Slow down," he said in his thick voice as he shaped the words.

Amanda looked at her feet, then raised her head and signed, *deaf*. She knew so little but he seemed to understand. His brown eyes were curious. She reminded herself that he was perfectly comfortable with silence. Maybe he didn't feel as strange as she did.

She formed *Y* with her right hand and ran it in a semicircle at her jaw. "Yesterday," she said, then paused.

Jake watched her struggle. He stared at her attempt at *yesterday*, at her concentration. He didn't want to think about yesterday, ever, but she looked so funny and desperate it was hard to stay angry. He crossed his arms at his chest and waited.

Amanda was desperate for some clue to what the boy was thinking. Had her sign for *yesterday* been wrong? Hadn't he understood? His mouth quivered. He was trying not to laugh at her! Embarrassment flooded her. What a stupid idea to try and communicate with somebody who hated her. She blinked hard. "Forget it," she mumbled, and turned to the woods.

Jake had gone too far. Guilt stabbed him as he watched her swipe at her eyes. There wasn't any sense of victory, not over somebody who was trying so hard. This time he went after her and she stopped.

Jake formed an *A* with his fist and circled his heart. *Sorry*. She was watching, so he tapped his chest with his thumb and repeated it. *I'm sorry*.

Amanda nodded. She circled her own heart with

24

her fist, repeating his sign. Maybe they had said it all.

He raised his index finger and made a quick zig-zag motion, then pointed to the barn. "Horse."

Amanda repeated the sign. "Lightning?"

He pointed to the sky and clapped his hands together until she laughed. It must be *Lightning*.

More silence. She held out her wrist and tapped her watch. "I have to go."

He signed again and she couldn't understand. She was getting used to the heat in her cheeks.

Jake watched the girl blush. She looked so uncomfortable it spurred him on. "Name," he repeated slowly. He tapped her chin and finger spelled. With every letter he watched her face for a hint that she understood. Her flush deepened and there was no sign of comprehension. He sighed and grabbed her by the wrist, relieved that she didn't pull away, then tugged her to the dirt in the paddock. With a stick he wrote at their feet: *JAKE HACKETT*.

"Jake," he saw her say with obvious relief. "Jake Hackett." She took the stick. *AMANDA ALDEN*.

Again he tapped her shoulder. He formed *J* with his pinky finger. He circled the back of his hand, *Island*, and tapped his chest. "J of the Island means Jake Hackett. Me."

"Show me Amanda," she replied, grateful that her face was cooling off.

Jake looked at her, at the barn and the trees and back at the opening in the woods from which she'd come. *A*, he formed for *Amanda*. *May*, he signed. He bunched his fingertips to either side of his nose. *Flower*.

Mayflower! Amanda groaned at the reference to

25

her ancestors and her reason for being on the island. He pointed in the direction of her house and drew the outline in the air with his fingers. *A. Mayflower*, he signed again, and then he grabbed her hands so she'd repeat it.

She did. *A. Mayflower*.

"Your name to me."

Your name to me, Amanda repeated to herself. She would have chosen anything but the Mayflower as her sign, but she was too relieved and startled to stumble through another fit of awkwardness.

She wrinkled her nose, and Jake was reminded that he smelled of the day's work. He tapped his own watch to escape.

Amanda nodded and moved her fingers in a wave.

He signed and watched her as she tried to understand. He signed, *island*, and outlined the house a second time. "How long?"

Embarrassment was her only reaction.

Jake shrugged it off and waved so she'd understand to leave. She seemed grateful. The minute she turned and started for the path, he went back to the barn. He lead Lightning into the paddock and was heading for the kitchen when a blur from the woods made him turn. She came back at a jog, right over to him, and grabbed his arm.

Amanda circled the back of her hand with her pinky finger. "I just figured it out! Island. You were asking how long I'd be on the island. All summer. My family's rented the house till the end of August. That is, part of my family. My parents are divorced and I'm here with my father . . ." She stopped in midsentence as he put his hand over her mouth.

Jake took his fingers away and watched Amanda

slap her forehead. Did she know it meant stupid? He laughed; she looked relieved.

"All summer," she repeated.

Jake nodded.

Amanda waited for more of a reaction. Was all summer good or bad? He didn't say. He just waved and headed for his kitchen door.

Chapter
4

At eleven o'clock the next morning, Amanda was back on the beach, in charge of her half brothers. Two boys under the age of eight were not her idea of great company. At the moment, Todd was tugging her closer to the shoreline, where Eric was waiting.

It felt as though she weren't a daughter anymore but a mother's helper.

"Watch the boys for a minute, will you?" her stepmother was always saying.

"Nancy and I would like to go for a sail, if you'll take the boys for a walk and make them some lunch," her father might add.

The real reason her father wanted her along for

the summer seemed obvious: She was a built-in baby-sitter. Noboby cared that she had her own problems and concerns — not that she shared them.

She reached a spot littered with horseshoe crabs, creepy and prehistoric-looking with their dark green, helmet-shaped shells. Todd bent over and she made a face. "Don't!"

Too late. He picked up the creature by it's thin, sharp tail and dangled it at her. "Neat, huh?"

"Don't be gross." As she spoke, she watched the waterline. There were no clammers in sight, no sun-bathers. Except for the three of them, and the creatures, the beach was deserted. She'd even looked for horse tracks in the damp sand but found none.

"This is my big chance," Eric was saying. "Dad says these crabs are as old as the dinosaurs, but they only come up on land for a short while. Next week they'll be back out in the water."

"Then you'll never get me in this bay," Amanda muttered. She wondered what the sign for horse-shoe crab was, and half brother, sailboat, and divorce. While the boys explored, she practiced circling the back of her right fist with her left pinky finger: *Island. Jake of the Island.*

Who lived in the house with him? She hadn't seen any family. Maybe he didn't really live there at all. Maybe Jake had a cabin at the edge of the woods. He was an orphan; his parents were buried in the cemetery behind Pilgrim House, and he'd grown up wild and alone. He lived on peaches from the or-chard and clams that he caught. He lobstered with the traps she'd seen in the barn. He had a campfire going at night, where he'd steam his day's catch and eat by firelight. Maybe Jake had never seen a girl on the island until he'd spotted her on the beach.

"Peanut butter and Marshmallow Fluff."

Amanda blinked. "What?"

Eric looked exasperated. "I said it's time for peanut butter and Marshmallow Fluff. Mom said after we explored you'd make us lunch."

"Whenever we got hungry," Todd added.

Two little sandpipers skirted the waterline. "Okay, okay, I'll feed you. It sure beats looking at these stupid crabs."

She marched the boys back up the bluff to the house and made them empty their pockets of shells, sea glass, and interesting rocks. They washed their hands under the old-fashioned pump at the soapstone sink, but when they turned the chore into a water fight she sent them back outside.

"Stay near the house and behave! Lunch'll be ready in a minute," Amanda commanded. When she'd piled a tray with three peanut butter and Marshmallow Fluff sandwiches, three lemonades, and a package of cookies, she eased the old screen door open and went out. The lawn was deserted.

"Eric, Todd, lunch." She waited and called again. When she didn't get an answer, she put the tray under a tree impatiently and tried to think like a seven-year-old boy. Back to the beach? Over to the cemetery? Into the outhouse?

The old wooden "two-holer" was closest, so she walked around to the back of the house. The outhouse door was slightly ajar. No brothers. Amanda looked across the back lawn to the underbrush and the towering beech tree sheltering the cemetery.

"I'm not in the mood for hide-and-seek, you guys," she yelled.

When she didn't get a reply, she walked to the edge of the woods and stood at the cemetery's decrepit iron railing. She called out again, glancing at the grave markers. *Hackett* was chiseled into a thin headstone and under it, *Joshua 1830–1897* and *Georgina 1835–1899*. Amanda's heart jumped. Had she noticed before, when the name hadn't meant anything? The dates on the headstone were too old to have been for Jake's parents; grandparents maybe.

Amanda looked into the deep woods on the other side of the headstones. Her brothers didn't know the paths any better than she did. Two little boys could be anywhere. The pine tops whistled in the seabreeze as she called them another time. The sound of the swaying treetops were her only reply.

Amanda was angry, then concerned, then angry again. They hadn't been out of her sight for five minutes. It wasn't her fault; she'd only been making lunch. She crossed the cemetery and went into the woods. The soft pine needles whooshed under her sneakers. Nature seemed to be making a lot of noise, but her brothers weren't making any.

The search was fruitless. The woods grew dense and pathless, too dark even for wild raspberries. There was no sign that two boys had charged their way into the pines.

She left and went back around the house, more worried about the dangers of the water than the woods. From the corner of the house she could see the bay and the distant white triangular sail of her

31

parents' small sloop. They were far out of yelling range, just the way they wanted it.

"Good," she muttered. If she lost the boys and gave Nancy and her father a good scare, maybe they wouldn't trust her with them anymore. Then she wouldn't have to baby-sit.

She couldn't see the beach below the bluff without walking to the edge of the front lawn. As she passed the tree, she looked at the tray. Two sandwiches were missing. Her concern vanished. Anger rose in her. "Okay, you two. This isn't funny! I know you're not hungry, and I know you're not lost or drowned," she yelled.

"Hey, Mandy," finally drifted up to her from the beach.

She ignored the relief she felt at hearing Eric's voice as she stomped across the grass to the cliff.

She stood at the top of the wooden stairs that wound down among the rocks. Eric and Todd were below, out at the water's edge, back with the horse-shoe crabs. Kneeling in the sand between them was Jake Hackett with a sea creature in his hand.

When she recovered from her surprise, she put her hand on the railing and went down the beach steps.

"Holy cow, we called and called you," Todd said.

Amanda's relief made her all the more angry. "Me! What do you think I've been doing? You know better than to come back down here without telling me. I've been in the woods . . . all over the place. Don't ever — " She stopped. Jake got up and dusted sand from the knees of his jeans. His serious expression made her unexpectedly shy. Once again she sensed his disapproval.

"I think his ears are broken," Eric whispered.

Todd elbowed his brother. "Deaf, stupid."

Eric pushed him back and Amanda stepped between them. "Don't call your brother stupid."

They all watched as Jake grimaced and bent and unbent his fingers in front of his face.

"Grouchy," Eric exclaimed.

Amanda looked from Jake to the other child. "How'd you know that?"

"Sesame Street," Todd answered for Eric. "It's the sign for Oscar the Grouch. I told you he was deaf."

Amanda smiled apologetically at Jake, still unsure of herself. "His name is Jake Hackett." She signed his name on the back of her hand. "Try it." Obediently, Eric and Todd repeated the sign.

Jake watched the girl sign his name. She remembered! He smiled and signed, *Amanda, Mayflower. Brothers?* He could tell she didn't understand. He repeated the tipping of the hat sign and then tapped his index fingers together. Finally she nodded and drew ½ in the sand at their feet. Half brothers, he thought and nodded.

Eric tugged Amanda's arm. "Ask him to do my name."

She laughed at his stage whisper. "I don't know how," she replied. "You don't need to whisper. Write it in the sand."

Jake watched as the boys wrote T O D D, then E R I C, side by side. He looked them over and thought a moment. He finger spelled *E* and added the sign for ocean. As he moved his hands to simulate waves, the little boy's face lit up. Jake pointed at him. Obediently, Eric repeated the motions, waited for Jake, then tried again.

Amanda began to relax. All morning she'd half hoped that she might run into Jake again, and all morning she worried about what to say if he did show up. She hadn't counted on the boys' enthusiasm or the fact that they were making it easier. She didn't feel as frantic or awkward. She watched them and wished she could be as open and unselfconscious.

Jake signed *T* across his forehead because Todd had bangs. The seven-year-old picked it up immediately and repeated it. The game started from there. The boys tugged Jake from item to item, pointing, waiting, and repeating the signs for ocean, lighthouse, sand, seaweed, even horsehoe crab.

Amanda watched without commenting. She'd never seen a boy as animated and expressive as Jake was when he communicated. He used his eyebrows, his eyes and mouth, he even moved his shoulders when he signed. And never had a boy watched her so intently when she spoke.

She stopped them long enough to tell the boys she was going to get the rest of the lunch. She went up to the house, made an extra sandwich, and returned with the drinks and dessert as well. All four of them settled in a sheltered nook against the rocks. She offered Jake the peanut butter and Marshmallow Fluff sandwich as the boys ate the cookies.

"Ask him what the sign for cookie is," Eric said.

"How about the sign for lunch? Ask him where he lives."

Amanda looked at both of them. "I don't know how."

"How'd you know he was deaf," Todd added.

Jake frowned.

34

"I met him on a walk a few days ago."

Eric moved closer to Amanda. "How come he doesn't talk? Is his voice broken, too?"

"Later. I'll explain it later," she mumbled between bites, not looking at Jake.

Jake clapped his hands together, making the three of them look at him curiously. *Hearing people*, he signed angrily. *Hearing people always talk as if we aren't there. I'm deaf, not stupid. I can read your lips, if you look at me. I understand! I can tell you these things! Talk to me; I'm a person, too. I hate peanut butter.*

Amanda felt herself blush. She recognized the swing of his fingers from his eyes to theirs: *Look at me*. The rest she didn't understand, but the meaning was clear. She made a fist and circled her heart.

Jake watched her apologize.

"Do what I'm doing," she ordered. Todd and Eric repeated the gesture. "We're sorry," Amanda said.

Jake shrugged. It wasn't all their fault. He'd walked up their beach. When he'd stopped to watch the crabs, the boys had come down from the bluff. He'd been okay until the girl came down the steps. The girl: Amanda. She made him self-conscious, and being self-conscious made him angry. Again he shrugged, then circled his own heart. He took a drink of lemonade and they all sat in awkward silence.

Eric looked up at Amanda. "Can't I ask him any more stuff?"

She pointed to Jake. "Ask *him*, not me. He wants you to speak right to him, Eric."

The boy nodded, tugged Jake's sleeve, and held up his Oreo.

Jake signed, *Cookie*.

The little boy repeated it, then tugged again.

"Talk to him, Eric, stop pulling his clothes," Amanda said.

"But he can't — All right." He looked shyly at Jake. "Show me the sign for lunch."

Jake complied. He signed, *Lunch, cookie*, and then continued with *boy, girl, rock, head, arm, leg, eyes, nose, mouth*, and *hair*. The boys couldn't get enough. When Eric held up his hand, Jake signed the word. He wanted to tell them he was more than a sign language dictionary, but the boys stopped. He watched Todd look at Amanda.

"You're not trying," Todd said.

"I'm eating," she answered.

"No you're not. Try to sign," Todd demanded.

"Okay, okay," she whispered.

Amanda got it wrong and Jake moved her fingers into the right position. As his fingers closed over hers, he moved her oversized signet ring.

She pulled her hand away. "Eric and Todd, sign your names once more."

When they'd finished, she added *Amanda, Mayflower* and explained to her brothers what the sign was for. The boys groaned and held their stomachs.

She pointed at them, but looked this time at Jake. "Watch out," she spoke clearly. "Jake can make your signs *Mayflower*, too."

Chapter
5

Amanda decided the boys had pestered Jake enough. When they'd swallowed the last of their lemonade, she ordered them back to exploring. However, as they left their picnic spot for the beach, Amanda had to hold back the urge to tell them to stay with her. She leaned back against the rocks and Jake did the same. Nervousness fluttered in her.

They sat in silence and watched the boys. As she tried to think of something to say, Amanda caught Jake looking at her ring again, but this time he tapped his ribs. He pulled up his shirt, made a fist, and pointed to a small, purple bruise.

She closed her eyes and hoped the sand would

swallow her. When it didn't, she looked at Jake. "I did that?"

He nodded, but unlike their first encounters, he didn't want to embarrass her.

She was getting very comfortable signing *I'm sorry*. Now what? "When I first saw you, I didn't understand about you, about your deafness. You scared me. Everything was strange." She stopped.

He nodded and they sat in silence again while Amanda wondered if he'd really understood. After a moment Jake tapped his watch. *I have to meet my father's boat. I'm going over to the mainland to help him with his catch.* He watched her mouth as she gave him a vague smile. She didn't understand. That was nothing new. He stood up and thanked her for the lunch. He didn't bother to apologize about hating peanut butter. She probably hadn't understood that, either, especially since he'd eaten the sandwich.

He turned and began to walk down the beach, then disappeared through the opening in the hedge roses. Simple and direct. She wanted to get used to it.

She hated feeling so confused, so unsure of herself. She never felt that way with Chris or any of her other friends. With Jake, she never knew what he was thinking until he got angry or she did something wrong.

Having the boys with her was a big help, but at the same time she resented their intrusion. Off the island, they never hung around when she was at her father's. But then, at home she didn't have a friend like Jake. She wasn't even sure the mysterious boy *was* a friend, not yet.

Jake's departure left a void. Amanda was back to baby-sitting. Why hadn't she asked about Lightning? She could have gotten a conversation going, something to make him stay longer. She'd never met anyone with such an aura of mystery, someone who just appeared and disappeared. He was like the island itself: Some of it was open and obvious and some of it was full of secrets.

Within the hour, Nancy and Bradford Alden returned from their sail. The boys went down the beach to greet them, and Amanda braced herself for Todd and Eric's review of the afternoon. Her father and stepmother had barely beached the sailboat when the boys began to jabber, sign, and regale them with descriptions of Jake.

Her stepmother and father looked at Amanda with curiosity and interest. She brushed it off. "I met him a few days ago on the beach," was as far as she'd go.

"Well how lovely to have someone your own age on the island. Maybe you'll finally have some fun. I hope you'll make an effort to ignore his handicap," Nancy Alden replied.

"He isn't handicapped. He just can't hear, and you can't ignore it," Amanda snapped.

It was Eric's idea to go for a walk and Todd's to gather raspberries. Normally — had it been as recent as that morning? — Amanda would have groaned and protested her role as responsible oldest child. She amazed her father by volunteering to take them.

They followed the path from the back of the house, and Amanda guided them toward the open field on the pretext of showing them Pilgrim Rock. All the while her ears were tuned expectantly to the sound of a whinny.

When Jake didn't appear on horseback in the field, Amanda let the boys wander ahead of her. Her heart pounded with nervous excitement as they followed the path to the Hacketts'. In her head, she practiced signing. In the end she didn't need it.

As it turned out, Jake had a hearing family. His mother had been in the back garden and introduced herself when Amanda and the boys got to the house. She welcomed them to the island and answered Eric's endless questions.

Amanda turned scarlet when Eric asked if anybody else in Jake's family "had broken ears," but Mrs. Hackett just laughed. She explained about Jake's illness. She told them about her daughters' normal hearing and added that one was married to a harbormaster on the North Shore and one was living and working on Cape Cod.

Amanda tried not to show how interested she was. Mrs. Hackett added that her son had gone into town with his father, who was a lobsterman. It was certainly different than the world Amanda knew, but hardly the exotic life-in-the-wild she'd fantasized for Jake. It was kind of disappointing.

Amanda had been surprised at how much courage it had taken, even the second time, to walk over the island to the Hackett farm. At home she would have phoned, or had one of her older friends drive down his street. Jake didn't have a street, and even if the island had had telephones, that wouldn't have done her any good, either. He couldn't hear.

None of her social rules applied here. You walked

where you had to go and carried a flashlight if it was dark. There were no malls where you might run into somebody to make it easier, no classes together. There wasn't even a store, just two little boys and raspberries as an excuse for a visit.

Caterham was quiet by the time Stephen Hackett nosed the *Sharon* to the commercial dock at the town landing. Jake and his father hauled the plastic bins of lobsters from the boat to the back of the family's pickup truck. While his father talked business with the harbormaster, Mack Howland, Jake added the empty bait buckets.

Jake drove the few blocks to the fish market and backed the truck around to the loading dock. Across the street, a knot of teenagers he recognized from school stood outside the sailboard shop. One of them waved; Jake waved back. Mistral and Windsurfer sailboards leaned against the building, their sails wet from the day's workout.

A girl with hair like Amanda's laughed at something one of the boys said. She cocked her head flirtatiously and put her hands in her hip pockets. Those would be the kind of friends Amanda would have, Jake thought; popular, rich, no troubles.

When he and his father unloaded the catch into saltwater troughs in the back room of the fish market and the paperwork was finished, the last leg of the day's work began. Loading bait was hard, smelly work. Fish remains were transported in barrels, trucked up from New Bedford. The lobstermen lined up to fork the bait into their smaller buckets at a nearby marina. With school out, Jake was one of three teenagers along. The other boys acknowledged him, then went back to talking as they waited in the informal line.

Jake stood and followed his father's conversation which, as usual, centered around the weather, harvest restrictions, or the rising price of bait. The air was pungent as the line shortened and they approached the open truck. June wasn't so bad. Come July and the dog days of August, the smell could knock you over.

He smiled to himself as he imagined Amanda "Mayflower" Alden's reaction to shoveling bait. He tried to envision her in knee-high boots, lugging the buckets. Mayflower, the girl who wouldn't touch a horseshoe crab.

His father nudged him. "Funny?"

Jake shrugged. *Nothing important.*

When it was the Hacketts' turn, they worked side by side and finished in half the time. With the salted bait in the back of the pickup, Jake drove the return trip to the town landing. Father and son loaded the *Sharon*, parked the truck, and with a wave from Mack Howland, headed back across the channel. By suppertime they were showered and ready for the chowder that awaited them.

For dessert, Sharon Hackett dished out vanilla ice cream and fresh raspberries. *You had a visitor.*

Jake looked at the fruit. *Two boys from the Pilgrim House?* he signed.

His mother glanced at his father and spoke as she signed to Jake, *"Two boys and their sister, Amanda. They brought us berries."*

Jake nodded and sprinkled some over his ice cream. He could feel his parents' curiosity. He ate a bite and with the spoon still in his mouth, he signed, *Nothing important.*

He lip-read as his mother talked to his father. "I thought Amanda looked familiar. She walked over here a few days ago." To her son she added, *I hope you'll make them feel at home.*

As Jake put Lightning in the paddock for the night, he thought that making Amanda feel at home was an intrusion. It would be much easier to leave her alone. It might be okay to run into her once in a while. But she got him all stirred up — angry one minute, self-conscious the next. Girls like Amanda did just fine, even on islands they didn't understand.

Chapter 6

As usual, Amanda awoke to the crackle of her father's marine weather radio. Two- to four-foot seas were reported from someplace foreign to her; the Coast Guard station at the Cape Cod Canal talked about air temperature at offshore buoys. The wind was reported in knots off Menemsha and Georges Bank, probably places fishermen went.

For the first time, she wondered if Jake's father listened every morning, if his day revolved around what was reported from Nantucket Shoals or Bennett's Ledge. If Jake were to be a lobsterman, how would he get the weather?

"Up and at 'em," her father called from the hall. "Tide's right and the weather's holding. Let's get a move on. This is our big day; she's gonna be a beauty." Amanda groaned and pulled the sheet up around her ears. Her father was a history professor trying to sound like a Yankee fisherman.

Since the moment she'd set foot on Clark's Island, Amanda had looked forward to getting off of it. It wouldn't happen often, unless her father scheduled an educational tour or groceries were needed. To-day's trip was the first tour and she'd thought about it all week. She certainly wasn't crazy about Pilgrim stuff, but at least it would get her to civilization.

The boys tumbled around in the next room, drowning out even the weather station. She didn't know which was worse. Amanda put her fingers in her ears. She stayed in bed long enough to imagine what silence would be like, to wake up only to the weather outside, the smell in the air, and the thoughts in her own head.

Amanda was about to give in to her father's sec-ond call, this time from downstairs, when Eric walked into the room. He tapped her shoulder and began a series of exaggerated gestures, none of which gave her a clue to what he was trying to say.

"Come on, Eric, you look stupid. Go eat and let me get dressed."

"You don't think Jake looks stupid."

"Jake's none of your business and neither is what I think about him."

Eric lifted his chin. "He can be my friend, too." He continued his signing.

"Todd, come get your brother out of here!"

Her second half brother appeared. "Don't be a geek, Eric," Todd said as he tugged him by the arm.

Eric slumped his shoulders. "You guys are the

45

geeks. I was only telling Mandy that we're going in the boat today to see some Pilgrim stuff."

"In what language?" Todd laughed.

"Finger language." He continued his protest as Todd tugged him by the collar and he followed his brother down to breakfast.

"Finger language," Amanda mumbled as she got out of bed. She tried to ignore the twinge of jealousy as she dressed. Eric was so open and natural with people, never shy, even with adults. Why didn't he know enough to be intimidated? Why didn't he worry about what a deaf person would think of him?

A Boston Whaler had been included with the house rental and the wide, comfortable motorboat was to be used for their excursions off island. That and the family car parked at the Caterham town landing seemed like the only modern conveniences in Amanda's summer, unless she counted the indoor plumbing and her boom box.

The day had been planned since their arrival. "This should be just wonderful," her father announced as they sat around the kitchen table. "We'll take the car from Caterham into Duxbury, see the Alden House and the graves of John Alden and Myles Standish. Maybe scout around a little, imagine what it was like to be brand-new settlers here."

"Let's not forget some shopping," Nancy Alden added with a wink at Amanda.

"Or the post office, so Mandy can get her mail," Todd added.

Eric made a big heart in the air with his index fingers and Amanda swatted him.

* * *

The family left on the outgoing tide with Dr Alden at the helm of the open boat. Both boys stood in their orange life jackets and watched the island shoreline with a shared pair of binoculars. A flock of gulls rose from the pines as the boat came around to the westerly side.

Amanda looked across at the mainland. Her anticipation wasn't as strong as what she'd felt at the beginning of the week, not that she wanted to stay behind. She wanted to see the towns, not the ancestral stuff that her father thought was so important. He had a way of turning everything into an educational experience. It wouldn't surprise her if her father required a term paper on the day's adventures.

Todd pointed to the open hillside on the island. "There's Jake's farm, Mom, where we took the raspberries. See the white house and the barn? He has a horse named Lightning."

As her father turned the boat into the channel and headed across the bay toward Caterham, Amanda saw Jake. He sat on Lightning, on the top of the hill, with the reins in one hand. The morning sun was at his back and he was in silhouette, like the first day when he'd been clamming. Amanda shielded her eyes and watched him watch their boat as they left the island behind them. Beside her, the boys waved frantically and yelled over the roar of the engine.

"Don't be dumb," Amanda complained. "He can't hear you."

"Oh, yeah, I forgot." Eric replied.

"Well, he can *see*," Todd added. "He's waving!"

47

Amanda squinted and looked back only in time to see horse and rider canter across the crest of the hill and disappear behind the thick trees.

The Aldens puttered into Caterham harbor at headway speed. Amanda stood next to her father as he called the harbormaster on the VHF marine radio and asked for instructions. Mack Howland directed him to the slip reserved for Clark's Island and they docked.

Amanda and her family visited the Alden House and the homesites of the other *Mayflower* passengers who settled Duxbury from nearby Plymouth. They went to the Standish and Alden graves, which sat in a plain little cemetery on a side street, and they ate a picnic lunch at the Myles Standish Monument in a park on Standish Shores. The boys talked Amanda into climbing the 116-foot monument, which gave her a touch of vertigo.

From the tower she looked east, the same direction as her bedroom window. White billowing clouds moved in the wind out beyond the lighthouse on the Gurnet. From her vantage point, she could see miles across Massachusetts Bay, nearly to Provincetown on the tip of Cape Cod. Clark's Island was a big green patch below her, Jake's house just a small dot of white. She could make out Lightning's paddock and the open field where Pilgrim Rock jutted up.

All kinds of crafts dotted the waters and, from that distance, she tried to spot some lobster boats among those headed for the harbors. She'd expected to be bored, not fascinated.

"We've got a tide to think about, children. Time

to pack up if you want some shopping in Caterham," Bradford Alden finally announced. He seemed delighted that they were enjoying themselves and were so reluctant to leave.

They returned to Caterham with just enough time to rush through the village street that bordered the harbor. Eric took to signing again, making up symbols for things along the way. "People are staring, cut it out," Amanda hissed.

Eric delighted in ignoring her. He went into the post office with his father.

"Anything for me?" Amanda asked with her best nonchalance.

Eric again made a heart with his fingers and shook his head.

"That's enough," his father said. "I'm sure you'll hear from Chris soon."

Amanda looked over the window display of shorts, Hawaiian-print shirts, and bathing suits at the sailboard shop. "Go on in and pick something out," her stepmother suggested. "I'll keep the boys busy."

When she emerged twenty minutes later with a pink flowered two-piece bathing suit and a sundress, the rest of the Aldens were nowhere in sight.

Amanda opened the screen door of the laundromat, looked through the window of the post office, and was about to head for the grocery store when Eric appeared. He was across the street, frantically waving at her.

"Guess who we found? Guess how we're gonna get back to the island?" The words spilled out as he tugged Amanda with him from the curb, around to the back of the fish market. Two pickup trucks were backed up to the open shop door, their tailgates down. A man leaned against one as he talked with her father, stepmother, and Todd.

Above him, in the truck bed, Jake Hackett stood by himself. He glanced at Amanda, and as she looked back, he turned away.

Chapter 7

The minute Jake had caught sight of Amanda coming out of the sailboard shop, he'd tensed. From his vantage point, up on the truck bed, he could see her across the street as she checked the shops, looking for her family.

Her brothers had spotted him, and her whole family was now chatting away with his father below where he stood. Silly. He'd watched Amanda leave the island; he'd known she was with them. He just didn't need to run into her here. Across the street would have been okay, at the grocery store or post office, but not at the back of the fish market, not like this.

Todd had gotten his attention, and now the little.

guy — Eric — had pulled his sister over to join them. They were all talking, all but Amanda.

Amanda looked as cool as his island woods. Her pink culottes were hardly wrinkled and her polo shirt was smooth. She tucked a strand of hair behind her ear in that way she had. She should have been somewhere sipping iced lemonade, not standing next to a pungent puddle of water that dripped from the burlap bags of mussels in the next truck. She looked as though every intake of breath was painful.

Jake watched as his father gestured and pointed to the harbor. They all nodded, spoke some more, and started off. Amanda glanced at him and he gave her a nod. At least he hadn't stared.

It wasn't until Jake got into the truck with his father that he understood what had transpired. The boys had asked and his father had agreed to take them and their sister back to the island on the *Sharon*.

Now Mr. Hackett swung the truck back around to their parking spot at the landing.

"A ride in the boat!" Jake spoke and signed for emphasis.

His father looked surprised. "Problem? The boys were thrilled."

Jake signed, *Girl. "She won't. Hates this stuff —"*

"Not a nature lover yet? I'll leave that to you, Jake. She doesn't have to come along."

The Aldens were waiting at the pier. Now Jake paid closer attention to the conversations. He lip-read his father's offer to check on the Alden's mail when he collected his own during the week; his request that the boys get into their life jackets; his mention of the Plymouth fireworks on the Fourth of

July. He was turning into a regular welcoming committee. Then he looked at Amanda and asked her to get a life vest, too. She didn't look too thrilled.

So she *was* coming along. Jake turned and lead the way down the dock to the *Sharon*. He wasn't sure he wanted her on the boat, not if she was going to hold her breath the whole time and wear that pained expression.

By the time he'd jumped aboard, Amanda was in the International Orange life vest. Jake motioned for her to come out into the sunshine, though the boys had to stay up next to the captain for safety. He leaned against the trawl rack to steady himself. Amanda gave the stern a good looking over before she leaned against anything.

You're too clean for the boat, he signed. *This is messy work.*

Amanda pointed to her culottes and Jake nodded. Maybe she understood and maybe she didn't.

They stood together without communicating. He watched her look at the empty plastic barrels that had held the catch and the hydraulic pulley that lifted the pots from the sea bottom. She looked at the foul-weather gear swaying from its hook and the box of claw bands and banding pliers. She glanced at her brothers up with his father and then out at the seagulls in the wake of the boat. He watched for signs of distaste, but she seemed mostly curious. He didn't know whether to be encouraged or not.

He was surprised when she tapped his shoulder. Amanda pointed behind them at the horizon. As she turned, the wind snapped her hair against her cheeks. The clouds swept over the lowering sun and dimmed the western light. Jake looked out at the green Duxbury skyline as Amanda pulled one of her hands up from the other. The monument? At 116 feet on top of a hill, it jutted far above the tree line, visible for miles in any direction.

"Myles Standish?"

Amanda understood and nodded. "We had a picnic. I climbed it. I could see your farm."

He tapped his chest and she nodded. She'd been looking for his farm. The wind blew her hair back again.

Jake could feel the onslaught of a headache from too much concentration. Usually it came from a long day of lip-reading and constant deciphering. With Amanda he had to decipher her expressions, her movements.

She hesitated and looked into the wheelhouse at her brothers. "The engine of your boat is very loud."

At that angle Jake couldn't read her lips. He touched her chin and immediately she faced him and circled her heart. *Sorry.* The engine is so noisy that if you could hear, I would have to yell. Loud! But you understood what I said and I only whispered. It's easier to talk to you than to my hearing brothers." She watched his expression. "I worry about how to talk to you. Are you angry?"

Jake shook his head. *"I worry too."*

Again, that small sense of relief danced around in her. He worried, too.

From the wheelhouse, Steve Hackett let Todd and Eric slow the *Sharon.* The tide was high enough to moor the boat at the pier, and he cut the engine as Jake put out the bumpers. With the engine noise reduced, the boys listened again in fascination to the crackle and fuzz of the marine radio, as boats all over the bay called to each other and to the harbors they were entering.

Jake nudged Amanda and pointed to the pier. "Out. Help."

She blanched. "Me?"

Steve Hackett cut the engine off. "Watch out, Amanda. My son'll have you hauling bait and pulling traps if you're not careful."

She jumped onto the pier and looked back into the boat. "I don't think — "

Before Amanda could continue the conversation, Jake took her hand and put the mooring line in it. He wove a figure eight in the air with his finger and pointed to the cleat at their feet.

"I don't think — " she tried again.

Hurry. I do the stern.

Amanda looked after him helplessly. She let him start and then copied the wrapping of the line around its holding mechanism, all the while trying not to get her culottes dirty.

When the stern line was secure, Jake clomped back to Amanda and looked at her attempt. He shrugged and signed, *Not bad for a girl.*

Amanda recognized the thumb-along-the-chin gesture and repeated it. "What about *girl?*"

This time Jake spoke. "Not . . . bad . . . for . . . a . . . girl." His eyes sparkled as he retied her line.

Captain Hackett ushered the boys ahead of him, off the pier, and up the hill toward home. Jake and Amanda followed, but she had to stop and face him each time she spoke. "You mean, not bad for a beginner. *Girl* has nothing to do with it."

"Girls can't handle line and boats as well as men." He fought a smile.

Amanda rose to the bait and sliced her thumb along her jaw again. "That better be the same sign for women. Women most certainly can handle line and boats as well as men."

Jake pointed at her. "Woman?"

He was teasing! She pointed back. "Man?"

Jake flexed his biceps.

Amanda pretended to groan. "I can do plenty of things as well — better — than boys. Better than you."

Jake shook his head and signed. *Not on this island.*

Amanda watched him circle the back of his hand. "Yes, on this island."

His heart leapt at how easily she understood. "What things?"

They'd reached the Hackett farm and she made a zigzag gesture. "Ride. I can ride Lightning better than you." Her heart pounded. Where had she found the nerve to say that!

Jake grabbed her hand, shook it, and pointed to the path. "Bet. In the field. Pilgrim Rock, half an hour."

Amanda was aware that the rest of the group was listening. "Bet. If I win," she tapped his chest and pointed at her half brothers, "you baby-sit for them the next time my parents go sailing."

Jake shrugged it off and replied in a flourish of signs.

"Chauvinist!" Amanda looked at his father. "What did he say?"

Mr. Hackett laughed. "Jake was only teasing. His sisters went out with me just as much as he does. They taught him as much as I did, too, maybe."

Amanda groaned. "What did he bet?"

"If Jake wins, you go clamming with him at low tide tomorrow."

Chapter
8

"Clamming," Amanda was still muttering to herself as she hurried her brothers through the
woods toward home. There was no way Jake would
get her out in the mud. "I'll win," she added as she
fended off Todd and Eric's enthusiasm and questions.

Back at the house, Amanda went up to her room
and changed into jeans. She came back downstairs
hoping she could leave without an explanation. Before she'd even entered the kitchen, she could hear
Todd and Eric. Not only were they giving their parents a blow-by-blow description of the boat ride,
they'd made sure to include Jake's insult and Amanda's challenge.

"Let's all go watch," Todd said as his half sister crossed the room.

"Don't even think about it," Amanda replied before the boy finished. She looked at her father beseechingly. "Dad?"

Dr. Alden nodded. "You boys stay here and help with dinner. It's clouded over and the wind's coming up, just as predicted. Listen to the lighthouse." The foghorn had begun to sound.

Nancy Alden asked where the riding would take place and Amanda described the spot.

"Brad?"

Dr. Alden patted his daughter. "Amanda, don't you be gone too long, either. You're an excellent rider but you're not to do anything foolish."

"I won't, I promise. Just let me go by myself."

"Chris won't like it," Todd piped in.

Amanda glared.

"That's enough out of you, young man," Mrs. Alden replied as she waved Amanda off.

"Ride safely," her father called after her.

Amanda hurried through the woods. She hated the fact that she had to explain what she was doing, that her family knew so much of what was going on. It wasn't like that with Chris. Both her parents knew his family and, as long as they knew where she was going and when she'd be back, they didn't get overly involved. On Clark's Island, Amanda felt as though she were under a microscope.

She came into the clearing and stood still, waiting. The breeze whipped around the open space, rustling the leaves and the pine needles. Jake finally appeared at the top of the outcrop and slid down off the rock to greet her. His hair was wet and his

59

jeans were well worn but fresh, like his polo shirt. Amanda smiled as she realized he'd told her half an hour so that he could shower and change. It made her feel good. As usual, Jake was watching her with those wide, brown eyes.

Jake tried to think of what to do next. Watching Amanda was a whole lot easier than coming up with anything she'd understand. It didn't occur to him that he might have been just as uneasy with hearing. *I like this place; I like to ride out here*, he signed.

Amanda's expression was painfully blank. They couldn't go on like this for the rest of the summer, and although she was embarrassed, she said, "I don't know what you're signing, Jake." With determination she added, "Show me how to say, 'I don't understand.'"

Did she mean it?

"Teach me more sign," she said very slowly.

Jake began with *repeat, say again*. He pivoted his right hand and tapped his fingertips into his left palm. *"Say again."*

She tried it.

"Or this way." He signed, *I . . . don't . . . understand*, and then took her hands. He looked at her fingers and helped her. Next he made her practice.

She copied Jake until she had it right and then added, *Thank you*. They looked at each other for a moment. "I'm sorry I don't know more. I'm sorry I can't understand you sometimes."

Jake read her lips. He was the one who usually had to apologize. Her sincerity made his chest ache. He didn't know what to say so he didn't say anything. He was thinking intently about something else.

Amanda tapped his shoulder. "Understand?"

Yes. He wished his heart would stop pounding so hard. Jake inhaled deeply and forced himself to speak. *"Who do you love?"*

Amanda furrowed her eyebrows. Jake's cheeks were flushed and she tried to imagine what personal thing he'd asked. She'd only make it worse if she made him repeat it.

Silence passed between them and then he took her left hand. Jake tapped her oversized ring and crossed his forearms against his chest. *Love.*

Amanda's eyes widened as she finally understood his bluntness. No one had ever asked her like that. Kids at school just knew she went with Chris. Was it love? "I go with Chris King, a boy in Lockwood."

Jake couldn't understand the name, but what did that matter? Of course she loved somebody, some-body off island, back in her real life. Instantly he pictured the boys at the sailboard shop, the athletes at Caterham High. "How old?"

"Sixteen."

Sixteen, like the guys in town who drove their fathers' sports cars or had their own. Amanda could have anybody she wanted. Jake moved his hands over an imaginary steering wheel.

"Does he have a car? Yes," Amanda said with a laugh. "Jake, there isn't time to talk about Chris. I came over here to win a bet." She cocked her head and tried to figure out the look in his eyes. Surely he didn't care whether she had a boyfriend, not when half the time he was frustrated with her and the other half they couldn't communicate. Even if she could sign fluently, she wasn't his type, not by a mile.

Part of the reason she was determined to win the

bet was because she knew Jake thought she was too prissy and proper. "How old are you?" she asked, to change the subject.

Jake signed, *Sixteen*. He was still imagining her boyfriend, some guy back home who never got his hands dirty. A boy who heard her when she spoke and understood what she said. . . . Never mind, what did it matter? He signed, *Lightning*. "Ready?" Without waiting for her reply, Jake walked around to the far side of the boulders.

Amanda hurried to keep up with him. It was hard enough when people changed the subject in spoken English. In sign, she got hopelessly confused. Apparently Jake didn't want to know any more about Chris, or maybe he was worried that it might rain before they could finish their bet. His silence made him seem moody, and she thought he was angry.

She turned her attention to the horse. The mare was tethered to a birch tree, nibbling grass. "Wait a minute, Lightning doesn't have on a saddle," Amanda cried as she took a good look.

Jake signed, *I'm deaf. I don't understand*, all of which Amanda recognized.

She pointed to Lightning's bare back. "You understand! Saddle, darn it! You did this on purpose."

Jake put on his best blank stare, but the corners of his mouth twitched.

Amanda opened her mouth to repeat it, then stopped as she looked at his expression. He wasn't angry at all. "Jake Hackett! Don't you tease me!"

"Sign, please."

She swooped her pinky finger into a *J* and circled the back of her hand. *Jake Hackett!*

She was getting pretty good. Amanda's unexpected effort and honesty were making him feel a little guilty at what he'd planned. *"Your bet, Mayflower. My horse."*

"No fair."

"Good. Give up."

"Give up, no way! *No*," she added with her hands. He'd expected her to quit!

He'd planned to call a truce, no baby-sitting, no clamming. He hadn't counted on stubbornness. "No bet." Two-word phrases weren't enough. He couldn't explain.

"Why, because I'm a *girl?*"

Jake sighed as he signed, *Not because you're a girl. Because if you can't ride bareback, you might get hurt.* He watched as anger flickered in her eyes. He should have known she wasn't the type to back down or give in.

Girl get hurt was what she understood. Of all the nerve. "The bet's on, saddle or not," she said as she marched past, aware that he couldn't read her lips at that angle.

The cloud cover had thickened over the evening light and there wasn't much time left to argue. They reached the horse together. Amanda looked at Jake. "Around the whole field. Trot, canter, gallop. Best rider."

Stubborn! *No*, he signed. Gallop would be too fast for her and trotting would be too difficult. "Canter only," he said slowly.

"Canter only?" Had she understood?

Jake nodded.

"Too easy," Amanda added.

"No. Hard enough."

Amanda decided to go along with him and she tapped Jake's chest. "You first."

That much he agreed to immediately. "Stay here."

She nodded and stepped back as he swung himself up on his horse. Amanda offered her hand and Jake shook it. "Good luck," she said as she looked up at him.

Jake let go of her hand, nudged the mare, and started across the field. He rode beautifully, and Amanda wondered if he took lessons. There was so much of his life she was curious about. Maybe there were things in her life Jake wondered about. Chris's ring had made him ask about a boyfriend. He'd noticed it; then again, how could he have helped but notice; she'd punched him in the ribs with it.

Distant thunder rumbled and wind whipped in gusts as Jake and Lightning set out. A tuft of grass flew up from the hooves but the horse's gait was smooth. Horse and rider moved together, over to the edge of the scrub pines that bordered the field, around the perimeter, behind the outcropping, and back. As Jake returned, he slowed Lightning down to a walk and then slid from her back onto the ground.

There was a lot more he could have done, but misjudging Amanda made him wary. If he were to show off, it might be just like her to try to match his antics just to keep up. Amanda was a lot braver than he'd realized, even if she wouldn't go near horseshoe crabs.

He was sorry he'd teased her on the boat; now he was responsible for her. He'd seen enough crazy behavior to know she was capable of recklessness.

He could just imagine her clinging to Lightning's mane, bouncing her insides to jelly as she tried to make it around the field. What if she fell; what if she broke something?

He imagined himself carrying her back to his house. He'd race across the channel for help in his own small motorboat and get Mack Howland to call a doctor. They'd return at breakneck speed. Or maybe it would be better to put her in the boat and get her off island.

"Okay, Lightning. My turn, Jake." Amanda interrupted his daydream by taking the reins.

Jake watched her. He should have found out how well she rode before he'd agreed to the bet. He should have thought the whole mess through. It was her idea to ride, but his stupid idea not to saddle the mare.

"Show me 'beautiful,' " Amanda said.

Jake opened his fingers and pushed his hands forward. Then he circled his face and closed his fingers — *Beautiful.*

Amanda smiled slyly. "Thank you, I will be."

He was too worried to laugh. *No jokes. "Bet's off. Don't ride. Doesn't matter."*

"You're afraid I'll win!"

"No." That wasn't it at all!

"Help me up."

Jake spoke as clearly as he could. "Don't ride just for the bet. Doesn't matter."

She was flattered, not that she'd admit it, so she brushed it off. "Help me up," she repeated, "I'll be careful. At least let me try."

There was no stopping her, so reluctantly Jake offered her a leg up. She stepped into his cupped hands and hoisted herself onto the horse. She hoped her smile looked brave.

Although neither of them knew it, their hearts were pounding equally hard with excitement and tension.

Chapter
9

Jake's doubt made his heart race. When Amanda looked down at him from Lightning, she was smiling and her blue eyes shone. He stared, as hard as he had the first day on the beach, looking for fear or doubt. She took the reins and nudged the mare with her sneakers.

Lightning began to trot; worry increased the pounding in his chest. Somehow Amanda managed to post enough to keep from slapping against the horse and then, when she was clear of Jake, she began to canter.

As he watched, he realized what she'd done and his worry melted once again into embarrassment. Her stride was smooth, every bit as smooth as his had been. Amanda rode bareback as well as he did! All the way across the field, around the edge of the meadow and back, she was in perfect synchronization. In no time, she and Lightning came around the rock and returned to the tree.

While the horse slowed, then stopped and went back to nibbling, Amanda smiled. She sat for a moment and caught her breath as she looked down at Jake. He looked relieved and surprised, but he was angry by the time she slid down to the ground.

Jake let her have it. He signed, *Not funny. You pretended to worry and all the time you could ride bareback just fine. This is an island, no doctor if you fell. . . . You made me responsible, just to get even. You set me up!* He refused to speak and enjoyed her confusion.

Say again, Amanda signed.

"No way."

I don't understand. How could she argue, defend herself, or even apologize if he wouldn't let her understand? She looked right into his angry, brown gaze. "You want me to be confused. You won't help. Say some words when you sign."

He tapped her shoulder hard with his index finger. *"You don't need help."* He walked past her, toward his horse.

"Hey!" This was terrible. She stepped in front of Jake and poked him, right back in his own shoulder, then bent and unbent her fingers in front of her face. *Grouch.*

Jake looked at Amanda in disbelief. Outside of his family, nobody argued with him. He didn't fight with hearing people because they didn't know enough signs to discuss anything as complicated

68

as feelings or differences of opinions. If problems couldn't be settled in *yes, no, I'm sorry*, arguments were abandoned and so, sometimes, were friendships.

Amanda repeated, *Confused grouch*.

Jake rubbed his temple and jammed his eyes shut for a minute. "You . . . don't . . . understand," he said.

"I know that!"

Why didn't she give up? Why wasn't she like other girls? *Forget it*, he signed. Complete thoughts were impossible and his head ached. As usual, nothing was turning out the way he'd planned.

For Amanda the silence was awkward but Jake's behavior was infuriating. Yes, she'd tricked him. Hadn't he tricked her? Oh, if only they could talk about it! She sighed so heavily, her shoulders slumped. Thunder rumbled again and she looked at the sky.

"What?"

She clapped her hands. "Thunder. Far away. The foghorn's been sounding at the lighthouse."

Jake corrected the sign with closed fists. "*Thunder*. Time to go home."

"*Thunder*," Amanda said as she signed. Even the weather was on his side!

Good-bye, Mayflower. Jake got back up on his horse.

Amanda frowned. What about the clamming and the baby-sitting? What a quitter! The sky flashed with faint lightning. Discussion, if you could call it that, would have to wait.

"See you around, Jake," Amanda said sarcastically. She started across the field to illustrate what she'd told him, as Jake nudged his horse into a walk and disappeared into the woods in the opposite direction.

Amanda hadn't gone more than a few yards when fat drops of rain splatted on her bare arms. She expected at least a few minutes of drizzle, enough time to get well on her way back to Pilgrim House before the storm. However, she wasn't familiar with the speed and power of ocean-born squalls. She'd gone only another ten feet when the sky opened.

The nor'easter swept across Massachusetts Bay, flattening the dune grass out on the barrier beach. The downpour whipped across the channel and over the island, moving in sheets as it swept over the field. Amanda was pelted with hard, driving rain, and it felt as though it were coming at her sideways. She gasped and pushed her hair from her face as she looked for shelter. Thunder cracked, this time with lightning just a second behind. She jumped. It was too close to even think about staying in the woods.

Her chest ached with fear but she started again across the open field, into the wind toward home. She was only halfway across the meadow when intuition made her turn around. Jake and Lightning — a gray, wet streak — were cantering through the rain toward her.

As he arrived beside her, Jake didn't sign or speak, he just put his hand down to Amanda. She grabbed his wrist, hung on, and swung herself up behind him. The grass was too slick to canter any longer, and the two of them reached the woods at a bottom-slapping trot.

Amanda managed to sit up straight until one more

clap of thunder cracked overhead. Immediately, she wrapped her arms around Jake's waist and plastered herself against him. He'd been in the woods and wasn't nearly as wet as she was; in fact, she was surprised at how warm he felt. She hugged him for all she was worth and they hurried on toward Pilgrim House.

The squall was violent but short-lived, and by the time the house was in sight, the storm had continued inland, over Standish Shores, pelting Duxbury and Caterham. The wind and rain dissipated into a light but steady shower as the horse and riders came around to the kitchen.

The moment they came into view, the four other Aldens pushed open the screen door and insisted they come in out of the rain. When they finally stomped into the kitchen, Amanda's stepmother handed them each a towel and Dr. Alden shook Jake's hand without speaking.

Eric wasted no time in badgering Jake to describe the thunderstorm in sign, making up his own words as he pleaded. "Show my Mom how to say 'lots of rain' and stuff, Jake."

"Leave him alone," Amanda said with an edge in her voice. "I'm sure he wants to get right home, too."

"I can sign with him, if I want. He's my friend, too."

"Tell him we're very pleased to meet him," Mrs. Alden said to Amanda.

"Tell him we appreciate his bringing you home," Dr. Alden added.

Going back through the storm for Amanda had been his way of apologizing, but Jake's mood wasn't any brighter. He felt like a creature on display. He did his best to ignore all the Aldens and he rubbed the towel over his arms, as if he hadn't understood any of the conversation.

Amanda had no trouble reading Jake's expression. "Please! All of you, talk to Jake, not to me."

Jake interrupted by tapping his wrist. *Time to go. My parents will worry, too. I have to get Lightning back.* Without giving anyone time to argue, he went out through the screen door.

Amanda glared at her family, but she was equally frustrated with Jake. She followed him outside. A soft, thick, misty drizzle was all that remained of the storm. The minute she reached him, Amanda circled her heart. *"I'm sorry."*

For what? Doesn't matter.

"Jake!" She spoke with frustration. "It does matter. What you feel matters."

He pretended not to understand. This girl wouldn't quit. She stood in front of him now, with her wet clothes sticking to her and her towel-dried hair beginning to curl from the dampness. Tiny droplets of moisture had collected on her lashes and he watched them as she stared at him.

Time to go, he signed.

Amanda grabbed his arm. "I want you to teach me sign. I want to learn."

"Why?"

"Why do you think, silly? So we can argue!" She laughed at his expression. "Oh, Jake, I'm kidding. So we *don't* always fight, so we can be friends. You can't leave until you show me the sign for *friends.*"

Friends! His heart thumped the way it had when she took off bareback. Was it worry, fear, risk?

72

"Friends, *understand?* Come on, Jake, I know you understand!"

Jake nodded and hooked his index fingers together and reversed his hands. *"Friends."* He watched her repeat it. She was still talking a mile a minute, so he put his fingers against her cheek and she stopped. *Say again*, he signed.

Amanda sighed. "I worry about hurting your feelings. I don't know what to say. I'm embarrassed to tell you I can't understand. It gives me a headache to guess what you're thinking. You're always mad at me."

Always mad? Anger wasn't half of what was jumbled up inside him. How could somebody who could barely communicate with him ever know what was in his head? Jake looked at his horse.

"Don't look away!" Amanda stepped around in front of him and signed, *friends*. "We need to work things out if we're *friends*." Finally Amanda circled her heart. "I didn't say I couldn't ride bareback, I just said I wanted a saddle. *I'm sorry*. I wanted to get even. You don't have to baby-sit."

Not funny.

Amanda understood the sign. "Not laughing. I guess I wanted to prove that girls can do anything boys can do."

He pointed at her. "Not Mayflower."

Yes, Mayflower! "I ride horses just as well as you."

Sorry, I'm deaf. Say again. For the first time in the long awkward moments, he looked as though he might be kidding.

"You know what I mean, Jake."

Jake's smile was slow and cunning. *You're a girl and you won't go clamming.* He couldn't help but

73

laugh. Every time he used the sign for girl, she looked incensed.

I don't understand, she signed. "And you know it," she added for emphasis.

Girl.

"Jake, I know that one!"

He formed *A* and made a semicircle at his chin. "Tomorrow." The rest he finger spelled. *C l a m m i n g.*

Amanda tried to figure a way out of the trap. "Lots of girls go clamming, I'm sure."

He pointed at her and shook his head.

"So what. I hate that stuff." She stuck out her tongue and made a terrible face, just in case he didn't understand.

Jake opened his fingers and made them tremble. *No. Frightened.*

"Don't be silly, I'm not scared."

"No?"

Amanda signed angrily, *No!* She thought Jake would sign back, but he raised his hand and ran it through his wet hair. Without another word, the boy got back up on his horse. He didn't even look down at her before he nudged Lightning and swung her around toward the woods and his farmstead.

Chapter
10

Afiter dinner, to chase the damp chill and the
humidity, Amanda's father built a fire in what
had been the parlor fireplace of the old house. It
served now as a family room. The adults and the
boys were playing Sorry at the coffee table, while
Amanda sat at an old oak desk and wrote to Chris.

Although there was no electricity, in the beginning of the century gaslights had been installed in
the walls. They smelled a little and gave off a soft,
steady hiss as the flame burned. Otherwise, they
were as bright as what she was used to in Lockwood.

The fire was crackling and the room was dry.
Outside, the foghorn sounded its ten-second warn-
ings from the bluff up on the barrier beach. It was

distant and froggy, almost comforting. She was getting so used to it, that she didn't even hear it half the time. The seagulls that circled and cawed all day long were quiet, but through the open windows, the steady moan of the wind in the pines was equally familiar.

All of this was Jake Hackett's world, whether he could hear it or not.

The Fourth of July was only days away and Amanda would be missing a pool party back home at Chris's country club. In the letter, she told him how she imagined it would be. She named songs she guessed the rock band would play in the ballroom. She told him she'd miss sitting with him, his arm around her, as he watched the fireworks over the golf course.

When she finished with all of that, she mentioned Jake. She'd meant to keep that part to a paragraph, but it was half a page by the time she'd described the past few days. Amanda eagerly told of her struggling with sign, how she wanted it to be a second language. She mentioned Jake's friendship with the boys, the family's ride in the lobster boat, and Lightning.

As she reread the letter, Amanda realized she hadn't mentioned Jake's age. She decided that was just as well; Chris might get the wrong impression if she mentioned that Jake was sixteen. She finished the letter with a weather report and the fact that there was nothing to do at night but play board games and read. When she'd added *Love, Amanda* and some *XXXXXXX*'s across the bottom, she sealed and addressed it. As she ran her finger across the flap, dismay stabbed her. She hadn't given a thought to mailing it.

"When can I get this to a mailbox?"

Dr. Alden looked up from the game. "I wish you'd thought to write yesterday, Mandy. We could have mailed it when we were in Caterham today."

"Can't you take the Whaler over again tomorrow?"

Her father looked out at the darkness. "Not if the weather's this wet. I'm not familiar enough with the channel to risk going through fog. Why don't we just see how things are in the morning?"

Amanda groaned.

"Don't worry," her stepmother added. "Steve Hackett offered to pick up the mail for us. I'm sure if you gave your letter to Jake, he'd see that his father took it over. Why don't you run it over to the Hacketts' first thing in the morning?"

Amanda was about to agree when she thought about Jake's reaction. Then she convinced herself she was being silly. Jake knew perfectly well what her relationship with Chris was. He wouldn't care one way or the other. He may have come back across the field to take her home, but her refusal to go clamming had clinched it, Amanda was sure. To Jake's way of thinking, she was just a squeamish girl from the suburbs.

At 7:30 the next morning, Jake Hackett sat at his kitchen table and stared at the sprig of mint his mother had put in his orange juice. It was July 1st, muggy and humid, which trapped the wet weather over the island. Everything outside was wrapped in the grayish fog.

Jake sat there intending to plan his day, but every thought was interrupted. His mother had left her book of American Sign Language on the table, after looking up a word. Just looking at the volume made him think of Amanda. She kept popping into his head: Amanda trying to sign; Amanda tricking him, arguing, kidding; Amanda riding like the wind. She was scared and prissy one minute and headstrong the next. It ruined his concentration.

Jake wasn't used to figuring people out. He didn't bother most of the time. The guys he hung around with during the school year were straightforward, regular guys. The girls he knew either shared his classes or dated his friends. He saw all of them in groups or at planned activities around town. Jake knew he intimidated people, girls especially. Most of them were embarrassed to make much of an effort to sign. Either he understood what they said, or there was no conversation. He was the one who had to struggle to communicate with his hearing friends.

None of them shared his island or popped in and out of his life the way Mayflower was doing. Now she said she wanted to learn more sign; she wanted to "speak" *his* language. His back tingled where she'd hugged him as they'd ridden through the rain, and he could picture, perfectly, the look in her blue eyes when she shaped words with her fingers. He could also picture the look she got when she was angry with him, and that's how he thought of her now — angry, frustrated. Why didn't she give up or keep her distance, the way the rest of his friends did? Why did she keep charging into his life? Why couldn't he stop thinking about it?

Jake sipped his juice. He signed *Mayflower* and

was tapping one bent index finger over the other —
friend — lost in thought, when he sensed he wasn't
alone and he turned in his chair. Amanda was in
the kitchen with one hand on the doorknob.

She had on rubber-soled shoes, and Hawaiian-
print shorts peaked out from the hem of a brand-
new, oversize, yellow slicker. From the walk over
the island in the mist, her hair was nearly as damp
as when he'd left her the night before, but she was
too far across the room for him to see if beads of
moisture hung on her lashes again. He was embarrassed that he remembered such detail and his
ears burned. The shock of seeing her made him
stand up.

"I knocked, but nobody answered," she said.

Jake tapped his ear and his chin. *I'm deaf,
remember?*

Amanda tried to read his expression. Was he kidding, sarcastic, angry?

"You do have two hearing parents living here.
Next time I'll press my face against the window,"
she added.

Jake grinned. *Mom, Dad, lobster boat, off island
in Plymouth.*

Amanda nodded. "Rats. I thought your father
might mail a letter."

Say again, Jake signed.

Wow! So far, she'd understood everything and he
hadn't spoken a word. Amanda pulled the letter from
her patch pocket to help him understand. "Letter."

Jake looked at the Christopher King in Amanda's
handwriting, then crossed his arms against his
chest. *Love letter.*

She made a face and crossed her eyes because

she couldn't think of what else to do. "None of your business."

"My business if I mail it," he said as he signed, to make sure she got it.

Not you, your father.

Gone to Plymouth.

"Never mind, then, Jake."

He put his hand up. "I'll take you."

Amanda stared to make sure she understood. "You and me?"

He pointed to her and himself. "To the post office." Jake's heart continued to race with the excitement of what he'd just proposed.

"Isn't it too foggy?"

"Off island is okay."

He watched as Amanda noticed the book of sign and picked it up. She ran the pages through her fingers. "Let me borrow this!" She tapped her chest, looked up *borrow*, and signed it. "Please, Jake. It's just what I need. Just for a few days?"

He shook his head and tapped his chin. *"My mother's."*

"She won't mind. Think how much I can teach myself. You can help me." Amanda looked at him and smiled. "You do want me to learn more, don't you? *Friends?*"

She'd seen him signing her name and that word and now she was teasing, he decided. "And the little boys, too," Jake replied. Somehow, adding Eric and Todd made Jake feel safer.

The fog was burning off, which improved the visibility. Amanda's father agreed to let her go, and her stepmother added a short shopping list. Dr. Alden also gave her a few postcards and a quick, unnecessary lecture on safety.

Jake's motorboat was about the same size as the Aldens', comfortable, roomy, and equipped with a VHF marine radio. Amanda stood next to Jake as they scooted across the bay and down the channel toward Caterham. They hadn't talked the whole way, but now, as Jake cut the engine down to headway speed, he tapped Amanda and pointed to the VHF.

"Me! I don't know what to do."

"Call." He added the signs for water and chief, which he used to mean harbormaster.

Say again, she signed.

Harbormaster.

"Jake, I don't know how. I don't know what you want."

They were gliding through the anchorage, skirting around the boats of all sizes on their moorings. "Never mind. Understand?"

Amanda nodded. He should have asked her if she knew how to use the marine radio. He should have told her what he wanted before they left the island. Now he was angry, and the unfairness made her angry, too.

Jake nudged the boat up to the town dock and the spot reserved for the islanders. Although it had been empty the times she'd used it before, two other, larger motorboats and a sloop were also moored alongside each other. The dock was bustling with people loading the boats with supplies and talking to one another. Amanda watched as most of them greeted Jake.

He waved back without speaking or signing, and when he'd cleated the boat, he indicated for

81

Amanda to go ahead of him, onto shore.

Amanda tapped Jake and pointed back. *Island people?*

Yes. "Most arrive today and tomorrow, for the summer." He hated the lump of jealousy he felt as he watched Amanda look at her arriving neighbors. A few days earlier, he hadn't even wanted her on the island. What was wrong with him, anyway?

As they walked through the parking lot, toward the main street, Amanda tapped him. "What did you want me to do with the radio? Tell me, so I'll know next time."

"Doesn't matter."

Amanda stopped. "Does matter. I want to help. I want to know what to do."

He should have guessed. "I wanted to tell Mack we were coming in, find out if *Sharon* has been in."

"How do I do that?"

"Mayflower — "

"Jake," she signed right back.

"I'll show you sometime."

"Promise?"

Jake finally laughed and crossed his heart.

In town, they picked up the groceries and mailed the letter. There was one waiting for her, addressed in a hurried, masculine scrawl.

"Read it," Jake said.

Amanda shook her head. "Later."

"Love stuff."

"I doubt it." She was dying to tear it open and see what Chris had to say after all these days apart, but she felt funny about doing it in front of Jake, so she stuffed it in the oversized pocket of her slicker.

82

"I told him about you," she added.

"All good stuff."

"What good stuff?"

Jake was quiet. He knew she was kidding, but he'd never expected her to write to her boyfriend about him. Sometimes it felt as though his sisters were the only girls he'd ever understand.

In less than an hour, they were headed back across the bay. Amanda would have liked to have stayed and mingle with the townspeople. Kids her own age were milling around. Some acknowledged Jake, but as he'd done with the islanders, he waved or nodded, but neither spoke nor signed. Since it was his boat and he was doing her a favor, she had no choice but to leave when he was ready.

Jake said they had to get going because of the outgoing tide, but she wasn't sure that was the whole reason. Under clearing skies, they raced back across the open water, splashed by salt spray, which glistened on their foul-weather gear.

Amanda could see signs of activity in the few houses that dotted the point of the island. There was a flag flying and someone was riding on a lawn mower. A touch of civilization, at last.

When Jake cut off the engine and docked his boat, she realized the lighthouse had stopped sounding its foghorn and she told him. He shrugged it off.

Had that hurt his feelings, since he couldn't hear it? Sometimes Jake seemed so locked inside himself she wanted to shake him. Amanda was quickly forgetting how intimidated she'd once been.

She stuck out her hand. *Thank you.*

He nodded.

"I owe you a favor."

"Call the *harbormaster* for me next time."

She imitated *harbormaster*. "I will." Since Jake seemed anxious to get up the hill, Amanda waved and started for home, along the beach.

Halfway up, among the wildflowers, Jake looked back at her. She was immersed in reading her letter, barely watching the rocky path in front of her.

The tide was perfect, the July sun was hidden by the clouds, and neither of his parents had given him any work before they had left. Jake pulled on his waders, grabbed his clamming rake and basket, and went back down the hill to his own side of the island. The thick sandy mud felt cool, even through his boots, as he waded into the silt.

Jake was up to his shins when Amanda appeared out of the scrub pine, back on the beach. What startled him this time wasn't her sudden appearance, but what she was doing.

As Jake straightened up and watched, Amanda took one enormous breath. Even at a distance, Jake could see the grimace on her face. Nevertheless, she marched toward him with her own rake and basket. Her sneakers disappeared into the black goo, which left a ring, like dark socks, against her bare legs. More than once she looked as though she might turn right back around, but she didn't. Slowly, painfully, she made her way across the mud flats to Jake.

Chapter
11

Jake caught himself. Laughing was definitely the wrong thing to do. Instead, he put down his gear and walked toward Amanda until they met halfway.

"Don't say anything, just show me how to catch these things," she snapped. She had changed into old cut-off jeans and added a pink sweatshirt under the slicker. The day they'd arrived, Dr. Alden had registered for three shellfishing permits, required for anyone over fourteen years old. She, of course, had thought she'd never use hers, but now it was pinned to her jeans.

Jake pointed to it. *"Pocket. It'll get wet."*

While Amanda fumbled with it, Jake motioned

her to follow him back to his rake and basket, another ten yards out. When he'd reached his spot, he stopped and looked at her again.

"Ready?"

"Don't I look ready?"

Jake didn't reply. She didn't look ready. Even in jeans and a sweatshirt, she looked out of place. She should be on a sailboat or shopping in a Caterham boutique, he thought. He'd known that she'd wanted to stay in town that afternoon, that she hadn't been ready to come back to the island so soon. He hadn't given her much choice, but he wasn't comfortable with her over there. He was barely comfortable with her on the island.

The Hackett mud flats at low tide was the last place Jake would have guessed she'd come to. Nevertheless, here she was, trailing after him. "Does this mean I have to sit for your brothers?" he asked slowly.

Amanda finally smiled. *Yes.* *"Fair trade."*

Jake shook his head. *"Not my idea. Bet was off."* He began to dig with his rake.

Amanda felt confused. She'd thought he would be impressed that she had tromped out to his spot to give clamming a try, but from what she could tell, he didn't care at all. He didn't care, and originally it had been his idea! Boys!

Now she stood next to him self-consciously, feeling as though she were in his way. It was too late to go back, so she watched as he disturbed the sandy bottom of the bay with his rake and then stuck his hands into the silt. He pulled up a four-inch soft-shell clam, dropped it into his basket, and motioned for her to do the same. She hesitated and he pointed at their feet. "Don't wait. Tide's coming back."

"Okay, okay," Amanda muttered as she took another breath and bent over. The bottom was mostly muddy sand so that her footing was firm. However, the exposed bed was littered with kelp, a few barnacled rocks, horseshoe crabs, and other things she had no desire to identify.

"Too stiff! Loosen up!"

Jake's muffled voice at her ear annoyed her further as she picked at a patch of sand.

Jake put his hands next to hers on the handle and realized she'd taken off her boyfriend's ring. He didn't give any indication that he'd noticed, but he added force to her effort by pushing the rake with her. "Dig in. Don't be afraid," he said without signing. He stood back so she could try by herself.

Amanda scratched at a patch of sand, but the tines of her rake came up empty.

Again, Jake signed.

Amanda dug again and this time Jake leaned over and sifted the muddy conglomeration with his hands. He found another clam and grinned as he showed it to her. He dropped it in her basket.

"Keep going," he added.

"Don't rush me, Jake!"

He looked out at the channel. "Not me. *Water.* Tide's coming back in."

Amanda looked out at the flat shoreline, half expecting to see a tidal wave rolling across the channel at them. The waterline was only inches closer, if that, lapping quietly. She went back to picking at the sand with her rake.

Shellfishing was strictly regulated and Jake's basket already held a quart of steamers. With a six-quart limit per family, per week, he planned to get the rest for the Fourth of July, still three days away.

He dug at the sand and pretended to work as he watched her. Why had she come out here in the first place? She looked as miserable as he'd ever seen her, as she scratched at the sand, grimacing and kicking aside the rocks with her muddy sneaker.

Jake tapped her shoulder and pointed to her hands. "Use your fingers, Mayflower."

"My rake's fine."

"Your rake is empty. No good. Clams are hiding."

Amanda brushed at her bangs with the back of her hand, not sure of what he'd said. "I know you think this is hilarious, Jake. Let me do it the way I want. You can go somewhere else if I'm bothering you."

"No bother." He went back to digging and threw a few more into his basket.

In the next half hour, Amanda managed to find four more clams. Once she'd raked them to the surface, she gingerly picked them up between her thumb and forefinger and added them to the others. The last one, as big as her palm, was a quahoag, and Jake took it back out.

"Too big, tough." He pretended to chew for her. "Chowder. Another time."

She made a face.

"Hate chowder, too?"

"Never mind."

Although she could have been more cooperative, she was so out of place, Jake almost felt sorry for her. He held up his open hand. "All done. Five for you. Enough to start. Melted butter — "

"You don't think I'm going to eat these things!"

Jake stared at Amanda, not sure he'd understood. He put down his rake so he could sign. *"Yes, eat them. Steamers. Wonderful."*

Though barely discernable, the tide was coming back in and the silty sand was getting wetter. Jake looked so shocked at the thought that she wasn't going to eat the catch, Amanda laughed. "I thought I'd sell my catch to one of the families who just got here."

No. Illegal.

Say again, she signed.

He pulled his own permit from his pocket. NO SHELLFISH TAKEN ON NONCOMMERCIAL PERMITS MAY BE SOLD, WASTED, OR BARTERED IN ANY MANNER. *"Your clams, for you. Mine, for me."*

"Jake, I was kidding. What's the big deal, anyway, if I did sell clams? Why don't you? Who's to know?"

Jake sighed. It hurt that she needed an explanation. What did she care? What did she know about the fragile balance in what was left of pollution-free waters? Girls like Mayflower didn't know about limits and depleted resources. If she'd been a Caterham girl, maybe she'd have been one who thought it was a thrill to steal lobsters from somebody's trap. What was a lobster here and there?

He couldn't make her understand. He told himself she didn't know enough sign; he didn't speak well enough. What if he did try, what if he did risk trying to explain and Amanda still didn't care? Which would be worse?

Amanda was about to ask if anybody ever came and checked the diggers, but Jake took her by the left hand.

89

"No ring."

"No ring? Don't worry, I didn't want to lose it out here so I put it on a chain around my — " Amanda patted her throat. "Oh, no!" She looked desperately at her feet while she ran her hand around her neck. "It's gone! The chain's gone, Chris's ring!"

Jake understood immediately. Amanda yanked her sweatshirt up, nearly to her bra, then felt around the waistband of her cut-offs. Before he could stop her, she knelt in the mud and began to rework every place she'd dug. The tide had added another ¼ inch of water and globs of the silt dripped through her fingers. Frantically, she pushed into the sea bottom up to her wrists. She squished it through her fingers over and over, in half a dozen places, desperate for the familiar feel of the big signet ring or the lump of tape.

Cold water rippled its way into the heel of her sneaker and sluiced under her foot. Jake finally knelt beside her and tried to put his hand on her arm to get her to slow down, but she shook him away. Both her knees were wet, and when she stood up the mud dripped in dark trickles down her shins.

Without looking at him, she retraced her steps forward, toward the beach. The water had yet to return there and it was easier to see. There was nothing in her path but the same creatures and bits of nature she'd stumbled over on her way out to Jake.

Jake tried to be useful and raked the wet sand as if cultivating a garden. He was sure they'd gone over every inch, and nothing appeared except more clumps of what they'd already dug. It made his chest ache to see her fight tears and to be so frantic. She didn't need him; there was nothing he could do. More than anything else, he hated feeling helpless.

If Jake hadn't said anything about the ring, Amanda'd still be tiptoeing around like a ballerina caught in a puddle. She'd hardly been able to touch the mud. Now, when she needed to find her boyfriend's ring, Amanda was digging for all she was worth. It hurt to watch her go to all that trouble. It hurt a lot.

Tears stung Amanda's eyes, and the pink of her sweatshirt was smeared with sandy mud. The silt drying on her bare legs made them itch and she smelled like the flats. She kept touching her throat as if she'd made a mistake, praying the chain was still there, after all.

The search was hopeless and she knew it, but she didn't stop until Jake finally put his hand on her arm. She tried to brush him away, but he leaned over and pulled her to her feet. The water was ankle deep.

"It's lost, Mayflower. No ring. Maybe tomorrow, next low tide."

"That's stupid and you know it. I'll never find it." She brushed the tears from her cheek and left a smudge like the ones on her sweatshirt.

Jake circled his heart but she didn't respond. She'd shut him out. She looked like she might lose her battle against the tears, so he turned away and picked up his gear.

Angrily, Amanda did the same. "This was stupid. Stupid, ridiculous . . . I must be crazy. I hate this stuff. How can you stand it? I hate everything out here, all this slime and dirt and muck and gross things on the bottom that you can't see. Look at my clothes! I smell awful! What a lamebrained idea."

She kept talking, her voice pitched with anger, as much at herself as anyone else. She didn't care whether Jake understood any of it, and when she stopped for a breath she picked up her basket and dumped the clams into his.

No, yours, Mayflower.

"Look, Jake, I don't want them; I never wanted them. They would have gone right into the garbage, 'waste or no waste,' " she said, referring to the permit.

Without responding, Jake took hers out of his basket and put them back in the water.

Amanda didn't bother to hide her sarcasm. "You wouldn't have even let me throw them away. That's the dumbest thing I ever heard."

"Not dumb. You don't understand. You don't care. Protection." He stopped speaking and continued with his hands. *Very fragile. Not much left.*

They marched back to the beach, where Amanda stopped, surprised that Jake had understood her. In the ten minutes since she'd searched for the ring, she'd shut him out and all but ignored him. Now she was surprised to see the anger in his own eyes.

"You shouldn't have come out here," he said as clearly as he could.

"Of course I shouldn't have! I only did it for you," she cried.

Had he read her lips correctly? He tapped his chest. "Me? You hate it. You won't eat them. Not my idea. Don't blame me."

The mud caked her legs and the itch was terrible. Her soggy, blackened sneakers stuck in the silt with every step. The slicker was hot and her sweatshirt was ruined. "I'm not blaming you! This is your world, not mine. I don't belong out here in this muck. Chris would think I'd gone crazy. Except for the ring, Christopher King would laugh himself silly, if he could see me."

"Chris, Chris, Chris." It sounded like "Kiss, kiss, kiss." Jake tapped his forehead with his fist and fought the wave of jealousy washing over him. *Stupid. "Stupid to come here with the ring. Too big, finger or neck. Too loose. Stupid."*

"I don't need a lecture! Don't you think I feel terrible enough?"

Say again.

"I don't want to — *say again.*" She paused and signed angrily, mocking him. "I have to repeat everything for you!" The minute she said it, she was ashamed of herself. Thankfully, Jake didn't respond and she hastily added, "I said it was stupid to come clamming, with or without Chris's ring."

"Yes. Stupid to clam. You hate them. You hate this."

"I can't understand you, Jake."

He took a breath and spoke again as he imitated her. *"I have to repeat everything for you."*

Amanda's face burned and she was embarrassed into silence, too embarrassed to apologize.

Go back to your own world, he signed. *Go back to things you know, and boys you know. Wear your pretty clothes. Lie on the beach all day or sail or listen to your boom box.*

Amanda nudged his arm. "Don't do that! Don't sign without helping me understand you."

"You're right, Mayflower."

"I'm right? Is that what you said? Right about what?"

"You belong with your Chris, somewhere else. You don't belong here."

Chapter
12

Neither spoke nor signed again. They picked up their gear and marched straight ahead. When they reached the beach, Amanda immediately kicked off her shoes and ran her feet through the sand, still damp from the rainy weather. It didn't help much, and she couldn't remember when she'd felt or looked so terrible. She was devastated, and she tried to tell herself it was only from the loss of the ring.

Tears kept welling up in her eyes, and she knew it was more than the ring — it was Jake's anger, too, that had her so upset.

When she'd stuck her ruined sneakers into her empty basket, she looked at him. He was watching a sandpiper, the picture of confidence. His polo shirt was still fresh and he'd rinsed his hands in a pool of water. His waders were only muddy from the shins down. His basket held clams.

His face was clean and the flush in his cheeks from arguing made his eyes the color of chocolate. Jake looked handsomer than ever, totally in his element, totally under control. Amanda was a fish out of water, muddy, and miserable.

Her head was full of things she wanted to say, but Jake's lips were tight and his jaw was set. He might as well have had a *No Trespassing* sign around his neck. She had to tap him to get him to look at her.

"When's the next low tide?" was all she said.

"Ring's gone."

"Just tell me what time low tide is, again! *Please*," she finished with her hands.

In his anger, Jake smugly signed. *First light*. He knew she wouldn't understand.

"Thanks a bunch," she muttered with a swipe at her eyes. Amanda spun on her heels, gear in hand, and marched.

Jake watched her go. He'd expected to feel triumphant, but he just felt mean. He put his hand out, but she never turned around. She just started back again for Pilgrim House.

Amanda felt Jake watching her as she turned and looked one last time at the clamming spot, now completely under water. She'd lost Christopher King's ring. He would never, never understand why she'd come out in the mud to dig for something she hated and wouldn't eat. The odd thing was, Amanda wasn't sure she understood why she'd done it, either.

Amanda got the information she needed from the tide chart, which hung in the kitchen. The next low tide was at dawn. She set her windup alarm clock for 4:45 A.M. and stuck it under her pillow. However, she was so anxious to get out of the house without her family knowing, she slept fitfully and woke on and off all night.

She planned to be back at the house before anybody woke up, but just in case somebody found her missing, she'd written a note saying she'd gotten up to watch the sunrise and walk on the beach. It would touch the frustrated fisherman in her father; he might even approve. With any luck, she'd have the ring back on her finger by breakfast.

Amanda awoke for good at twenty minutes till five and turned off the alarm before it rang. The sun, from her window, hadn't yet inched up out of the Atlantic, but the sky had lightened to a pale gray.

The Massachusetts coast was hundreds of miles further east than Pennsylvania and she was surprised at how bright it was, so early. New England summer mornings were brisk. Amanda shivered as she pulled on a maillot bathing suit, something she could wash the mud out of easily, by hand. The thought of the mud on her bare legs gave her gooseflesh and she made a face as she dressed.

Someday she'd tell Chris all about the fiasco, someday when the ring was safe and secure on her left hand again. She was either desperate for the ring or devoted to him, she decided, as she pulled two clean sweatshirts over her head. Nothing else could make her do anything this nuts.

Jake had been right about one thing: It was stupid to have worn the ring on a thin gold chain. Amanda made a fist and touched her forehead. *Stupid*. She caught herself and stood still. She'd signed without thinking about it.

Amanda looked in the mirror and signed again. This time: *Friends? Not friends?*

It seemed to her that every antique floorboard in the house squeaked under her bare feet. She grimaced all the way down the stair risers and took the biggest strides possible through the parlor and into the kitchen. She didn't dare use the bathroom, open a cupboard, or the bread box. She left her note on the table and it was all she could do to get the screen door open wide enough to slide through.

Since their arrival, Todd and Eric had tried unsuccessfully to get her to use the outhouse. Now Amanda tiptoed over to the little building. Never, in her wildest dreams, would she have thought this moment would come, but it had. All in the name of love for Chris and desperation for the return of the ring. Much to her surprise, using the "two-holer" wasn't bad at all.

Amanda Alden had used an outhouse, ridden in a lobster boat, clammed. . . . She began to laugh. Nobody in Lockwood would believe it, least of all Chris.

Clark's Island was bathed in the gray-green first light of day, as if it were overcast. In the five minutes it took to walk over the paths, the sky lightened as the sun rose. It came up behind the barrier beach as she scurried through the scrub pine and down to the Hacketts' side.

Above her, in the pines, the gulls came to life, screeching along with jays. A mockingbird flew up from the raspberry canes as Amanda came into the clearing at the top of the bluff. This wasn't an hour at which she was used to being up, and everything seemed new. The only time she'd ever been awake at dawn was on an occasional sleepover, when the gray light made her feel kind of sick and exhausted.

She slowed down to follow the sandy path down the hill, to the beach. There wasn't a breath of wind, no sounds of traffic, no voices, just cool quiet. Suddenly, the low gurgle of an engine made her look north.

One hundred yards away, the *Sharon* floated on her deep-water mooring. Diesel smoke and bubbles gurgled at the stern and Amanda could make out a figure in the wheelhouse. As she watched, a second figure squatted down at the bow, then stood up.

With the mooring line in his hand, Jake walked along the coaming. He jumped lightly into the wheelhouse with his father, and the lobster boat nosed into the channel with its trawl rack piled with traps.

Amanda forgot her hurry and watched until the sound was muffled and the boat was well away.

At that moment, Jake's life seemed exotic and unreachable, something he was reluctant to share and didn't want her to be a part of. He was so different from Chris — from any boy back home — so mysterious, so self-reliant. She imagined him out on the water all day, loading traps, taking the catch out. He stayed in shape, not from tennis or soccer, but hard work.

He had so much skill and confidence, he hardly seemed sixteen. Girls probably fell all over him. He probably went to a school for the hearing impaired, with girls who could sign anything, girls who understood him and didn't get confused or embarrassed. His kind of girl ate clams, knew all about boats, and didn't make a fool of herself. A wave of sadness washed over her. Jake was right — she didn't belong here.

The sun continued its inching into the sky, and beams of light filtered through the pines behind her. Out in front of her, the mud flats glistened, wide and bare, reminding her of what lay ahead.

Amanda groaned and the sadness deepened. Chris would be furious. He'd probably never speak to her again. She couldn't let that happen. She didn't want anything to go wrong between them. Every girl in Lockwood wanted to date Chris King, and she was the lucky one.

She had no choice but to search until she found his ring. She slid down the bluff on her bottom and heels, and then looked at the shoreline to make sure she went out onto the flats in the same spot as the afternoon before.

On the dry sand, at the spot where she thought she should begin, there was a lump of something army-drab-colored and folded. She put down her sneakers and rake and picked it up. It was a pair of waders. Jake's, she thought, left behind yesterday.

Amanda furrowed her eyebrows. They weren't Jake's. They were smaller, even a slightly different color and style, and they were much closer to her own size. She looked for a note or a name on the label. *Sharon Hackett* was scrawled in marker across the inside of the bib.

Amanda assumed Mrs. Hackett had gone clamming and left them. She also assumed that under the circumstances, Jake's mother wouldn't mind if Amanda borrowed them. She'd be careful and leave them just as she'd found them.

Of course, there was the distant possiblility that Jake had left them there for her. But he'd made it clear that the idea of searching again was stupid. Amanda scoffed at herself for considering it.

Amanda looked up the empty beach and finally pulled the waders on over her bathing suit. Would she ever understand what went on behind those deep, pensive eyes of his?

Jake found the waders at three o'clock. His peace offering lay folded where he'd left them, just above the high-water mark, off the flats. The tide was going out again and any trace of footprints had long since been washed away. He ignored the waders as he pulled off his work shirt, rubberized boots, and socks. Either Mayflower had been too angry to use them or she hadn't come back at all.

Even alone, it embarrassed him to think that he'd half expected to find her waiting gratefully on the pier when the lobster boat returned.

In his head, he'd worked it all out. She'd used them and returned them to the house. His mother would then tell her the time he'd be back on the island. He'd imagined himself consoling Amanda as she admitted the ring was gone for good. In his fantasy, somehow, Christopher King was gone along with it. *Stupid*, he signed. He was thinking like a kid. Better not to think about it at all, better not to let any of it get to him.

Jake stripped down to his jeans, started for the water, and was shin deep when he remembered his wallet and sunblock in his hip pocket. He tossed them back onto the sand and waded out until he could float in the chilling saltwater.

This was his self-prescribed remedy against frustration. He drifted on his back, avoiding the eel grass beneath him, forcing his mind to stay blank. Overhead a gull shot into the air and dropped a mollusk from its beak, then dove down to the rocks to devour it. Three snowy egrets were perched in the overhanging trees. Jake rolled over and swam a few strokes until he was too cold to stay in any longer.

He came out of the water shivering and refreshed. It was still over eighty degrees, hot enough to let the air dry him. He balled his shirt and socks into his boots, and it wasn't until he picked up the waders that Jake realized they had been used. Dried mud still caked the feet. Mayflower had come back to search, after all. Automatically he turned and looked out at the clamming spot.

It was impossible to keep his mind empty, but he no longer imagined himself consoling her. Amanda, desperately digging, grubby, tear-stained, intruded into his thoughts. He saw Amanda turning up her nose at his work, and Amanda patting her throat with her dreamy expression, expecting to feel her boyfriend's ring.

Stupid girl, he signed to himself.

Chapter
13

Jake had his arms full when he remembered his wallet. He swore to himself, dropped everything, and looked around. He hadn't paid much attention to where he'd thrown it and now he regretted it.

It took ten minutes, but he finally found it at the edge of some vegetation, which he moved aside with his bare foot. Something pressed into the arch as he shifted in the hot, dry sand under the beach roses. A thin gold chain caught between his toes. Jake leaned over, amazed, and picked up Amanda's ring.

Sand drifted between his fingers as he looked at the CGK monogram on the masculine gold ring. The adhesive tape was covered with granules of sand

and the clasp on the chain was broken. He turned the ring over slowly in the palm of his hand and then wedged it into the wet right front pocket of his jeans.

An hour later he stood in the drying yard, hosing down the waders and his jeans, which he'd pinned to the clothesline. He'd showered, changed into khaki shorts, and fed and watered Lightning, when Amanda suddenly appeared from the side of the house in a bright fuchsia bathing suit. She looked very startled, as if she might turn and run. He turned off the hose.

"I thought you were out on the boat." *Boat*, she signed.

"Came back." Jake cocked his head. Her eyes were puffy, rimmed with red, without a trace of makeup.

Mother? she signed and looked around.

Boat, he signed.

Amanda pointed to the waders. "She left them on the beach and I borrowed them. Will you thank her?" *Thank your mother.*

She stared at Jake's unreadable face, glad that she hadn't asked if he'd left the waders. What a dumb thought! Say something, she wanted to scream at him. Are you sorry for refusing to tell me when the next low tide was? Do you feel bad about telling me I don't belong here? But the questions remained unasked, and Jake turned the hose back on.

She tapped his shoulder. "I need to use them again so I don't ruin my new bathing suit. I hope your mother won't mind."

Mayflower, don't, he signed. How could she think

104

his mother had left the waders? Hadn't it occurred to Amanda that he'd put them there, that he'd meant them as an apology? He was about to explain that he'd found the ring, when she put both hands on her hips.

"Jake, I'm sorry you don't understand how important this is. Chris trusted me with his ring. It's a symbol — " She waved her hand. "Oh, never mind."

Anger filtered into his expression. *Never mind, why never mind? Because you think I don't understand? Because it's too much work to explain?*

Angrily, Amanda took the waders off the clothesline. "That's a trick of yours, isn't it?"

"What trick?"

"You know very well, Jake. When you're really ripped at somebody, you sign. You think I won't understand, so you just sign with your hands, on purpose. Well, watch out. I've got your book and I'm learning. I just might surprise you. Maybe I know exactly what you signed. And maybe the next time I feel like you, I'll turn my back and talk so you can't read my lips. Then we can both act like five-year-olds." Without another word, she left for the beach.

Five minutes later Jake followed and stood unobserved on the bluff above his family's beachfront. Let her stew over the stupid ring! He didn't care. In the ill-fitting waders, Amanda stumbled around the tidal flats below him. He watched her go over and over the area they'd first dug, first with a rake and then with her bare hands. She swatted at sand fleas and gnats, and left black, mucky handprints on her shoulders. Her energy lagged as the search remained futile and the tide lapped its way back around her ankles.

The meanness Jake had felt the day before, when he'd deliberately confused her by signing *first light*, was nothing compared with the guilt enveloping him now.

He desperately wanted not to care. He'd wanted to enjoy seeing her miserable and grimy. She'd invaded his island, invaded his thoughts, practically taken over his life. She was threatening in ways he couldn't quite grasp or control. All she cared about was her dumb boyfriend and his stupid ring.

Jake thought he would have a sense of satisfaction in watching her fumble with old waders and ruin an obviously expensive bathing suit, so he stood back and watched. Sometimes it felt as though he spent his whole life standing back and watching, never really being a part of anything.

Suddenly he hated himself for keeping the ring. He hadn't meant to keep it, hadn't planned on it, but that didn't matter. Amanda slowly clomped back up to the dry sand and sank down. She lowered her head, and even from that distance he could tell she was crying. She sat there for a long time, swamped in sadness he'd made worse.

Jake turned away and walked to the paddock, painfully aware of how devoted she was to a boy from another world; how far she'd go to find the ring that symbolized their relationship.

As abruptly as Jake had walked into Amanda's life, he left it. She returned the waders to an empty house and didn't see him again for two days. She assumed he went out lobstering, but she didn't ask. She didn't want to see him. She was tired of thinking about him and struggling and feeling self-conscious.

Stephen Hackett stopped by with mail for her father and reminded the family of the Fourth of July party. He didn't mention his son. Todd and Eric had made friends with the handful of children who were now in the other cottages, and they were too busy to pester her. They forgot about signing and left her alone.

Amanda spent her time on her own beach, on her own side of the island. She paged through the book of signing, took long, solitary walks, sometimes bringing home a bluejay feather or a bunch of wild-flowers for her room. She watched the boats out in the channel, and the nesting egrets, and tried to accept the fact that Chris's ring was gone for good. She understood the term "heavy heart." Hers really ached, all the time.

She wrote a long, rambling letter to Chris. Her melancholy feelings made her poetic, and she described to him her walk at dawn, the beauty of the island sunrise, the birds and their morning sounds, the departing lobster boat.

Of course she never mentioned why she'd been up so early. She wrote that she wished Chris could be with her, that the island was beautiful and mysterious, full of things she was just beginning to understand.

When she'd signed it with kisses along the bottom, she read it over. All her descriptions made her think of Jake, not Christopher. "How ridiculous," she mumbled to herself.

The Fourth of July dawned hot and clear. Amanda dressed in her new bathing suit and an oversized shirt, while the weather radio crackled its fair weather forecast from her father's room.

She had forced herself not to talk about her troubles. She had tried to forget about how awful Jake had made her feel and how she missed Chris, but she was so cranky sometimes, she fought with everybody.

At noon, two towheads appeared at the door with fists full of little American flags. Her father and stepmother left with them, happy to be away from Amanda for a while. She watched them carry towels and sand chairs back along the rocky beach to the party.

By the time Amanda walked down to the site on the southern tip of the island, the party was in full swing. The cottages that had been closed the last time she walked on the beach were flying red, white, and blue bunting over their doors. Croquet, volleyball, and horseshoes were set up on the beach, and inner tubes and floats were on the sand, along with a sailboard. A knot of girls and boys were jumping on skim boards and making them shoot along the waterline, and two adults were organizing a sand castle contest.

It wasn't the Lockwood Country Club, not by a mile. A whole day of hokey kids' stuff didn't have much appeal. Todd and Eric were busy with the floats and their new friends. Even Amanda's parents were right at home with the islanders, chatting away as if they'd summered there forever.

Safely off to the side, a heaping pile of seaweed lay steaming on the sand. Jake was there by himself, in a Celtics T-shirt and his khaki shorts, counting out ears of unshucked corn. Seeing him again made Amanda feel as unsure of herself as the first day on the beach. He didn't look up and Amanda told herself it didn't matter.

Body language and facial expressions said as much to Jake as any verbal conversation. Amanda was standing by herself, self-consciously touching her hair as she looked over the party. Under her loose shirt, he could see the same bathing suit she'd gone clamming in. She looked much better than the last time he'd seen her, but the sadness in her eyes was unmistakable. She was doing her best to look bored, but he knew better. He watched his mother welcome her and then turned away.

For two and a half days, Christopher King's ring had burned in Jake's conscience. He had it with him, and just tapping his pocket made him feel as though he were too close to the coals he was tending.

At sea, at the market, loading bait, and now adding corn to the clambake, he'd devised ways to return it. He'd thought and rethought his approach, never intending to take so long. The problem was that he was a lousy liar. But he'd made Amanda miserable, all right, and it had haunted him for nearly three days.

He tried to concentrate on the corn, but as he put the last ear under the seaweed, a familiar pair of legs appeared next to the steaming pit. Jake raised his head. Amanda's eyes were wide and blue, and her face was a mask of tension. She didn't sign.

"Your mother wants us to bring two coolers down from the barn."

Jake turned around.

From across the sand, his mother grinned slyly

and signed, *Pretty Mayflower. Go for it!*

"What did she say?"

Jake shrugged and looked disgusted.

"She's referring to me; I recognize my sign. I'll look up the rest."

That would be just like Mayflower, Jake thought. He brushed off the sand and started for the path, not at all sure that anybody really needed two more coolers.

Amanda trotted after him until she caught up. She was on the same side of him as the ring, and Jake put his hand in his pocket while he tried to think.

Once they were by themselves, off the sand and through the beach plum, Amanda slowed down. When Jake finally looked at her, he realized she'd been deep in thought, too. He watched her take a long breath.

"I thanked your mother, but she didn't know anything about her waders being on the beach."

He took his hands from his pockets and started to sign.

"Don't interrupt! I need to apologize. I'm sorry." *I'm sorry, Jake.* "Obviously, you left them there for me to use. I guess that was your way of apologizing and I made it worse."

Jake tried to shrug it off.

When he didn't respond, Amanda locked her bent index fingers. *Friends?*

Jake was beyond signing or speaking. Before he lost his nerve, he pulled the ring from his pocket and opened his hand.

She didn't move. She hardly breathed. Finally Amanda pressed her hands against her cheeks and stared at his palm and then she was staring at him.

Her fingers brushed over his hand as she took the ring. She was so close he could see tears fill in on her bottom lids and spill onto her lower lashes.

At first she tried to stay composed. "Where did you find it?" she asked, but she seemed to be choking and laughing. "I can't believe you went back and looked for it! I can't believe you found it!" *Thank you!* "Jake, you're wonderful." *Wonderful!*

Jake's flush deepened. She was signing and laughing and trying to control herself. Impulsively, he touched her cheek and wiped her tears, tripping slightly.

He'd only meant to keep his balance, but as he put his arm around her, she seemed to dissolve against him in tears. He didn't dare move; he didn't want to. When he tried to get her to look at him, Amanda broke into soft sobs, with her face pressed so hard against his chest, Jake was sure she could feel his heart hammering.

It was pounding against his ribs and he could feel Amanda mumbling into his shirt. He had no idea what she was saying. It didn't matter. He could have stood there forever, one hand across her shoulder, the other lost in the blonde hair at the back of her head.

"Oh, Mayflower." He spoke into the top of her hair. With the ring and chain in her fist, she held onto him as tightly as she'd hugged him when they'd ridden Lightning through the tunderstorm. Tears or not, it felt just as wonderful. They didn't talk or move and Jake didn't think. Any confession about the ring was long gone.

He waited until she'd cried herself out, hardly daring to think about how incredible she felt in his

111

arms. At last Amanda sighed against him. She raised her head and patted the damp smudges on his T-shirt apologetically. Her eyes were clear, as blue as the bay in the morning, and remnants of tears held her lashes in tiny triangles.

Before she moved another inch or he came back to reality and lost his nerve, he leaned over. He cupped her chin, and when she'd closed her eyes. he kissed her.

Chapter
14

Jake had dreamed of this moment in a thousand ways with a dozen girls. He'd thought about kissing daughters of his parents' friends, girls in his class he'd had crushes on, even the ones who dated the guys he hung around with, but he hadn't thought about any of them as much as he thought about kissing Amanda.

He'd gotten lost in the way she felt in his arms. She'd held onto him so tightly, he could feel her relief as she cried. For the moment, he ignored the reason and didn't think about the ring. He didn't think about anything but the happiness surging through him.

This was Mayflower, flesh and blood, not a dream.

Her hair tangled over his fingers and her shirt moved under his hand. Her mouth was salty where a tear had stopped and sweeter than he had imagined. In his arms she felt solid and soft, an incredible combination.

Amanda didn't move for a long time. Two seconds earlier she'd been too embarrassed by her uncontrollable crying to look at him, but her tears were from happiness. It flooded through her, pushing away everything else until kissing Jake Hackett felt like the most natural thing in the world, as if she'd expected to do it all along. He smelled faintly of charcoal and steamy kelp, of the clambake and the island. She was disturbed and awed by her own emotions, because deep down she knew it was more than gratitude that made her snuggle against him.

They sighed together and smiled shyly until Amanda looked away. She glanced at the ring in her hand as if it would force her to clear her thoughts. Somebody had to say something, so she signed, *Thank you, Jake. You're wonderful*.

Amanda didn't know how to convey the confusion she felt and she tried to tell herself it had just been a grateful kiss. She thought about the girls she'd imagined Jake knew on the mainland, how different his life must be once he got back in school. Suddenly she wanted him to have somebody special somewhere else; then they'd be even. Then she wouldn't feel the twinge of guilt that was stabbing at her.

Common sense told her she'd better change the mood, so she started up the hill toward the Hacketts' barn, but just having Jake walk beside her made the air electric.

She stopped only long enough to look at him so he could read her lips. "Where did you find Chris's ring?"

"Scrub pine, where the path opens. This morning. Clamming for picnic." A deep flush washed over Jake's face as he stumbled with the explanation. Amanda assumed it was from having to speak so slowly and repeat himself so she could understand him.

She put the ring in her pocket and smiled at him, then crossed her fists against her heart. *Love.* "Do you have a girlfriend at your school? Who do you love, Jake?"

Who did he love? Her question felt like a slap, but he said, "Lots of girls," and Amanda laughed.

"And they can sign, I bet," she replied.

Say again.

"Your girlfriends at your school know how to sign, how to talk to you better."

"No signing."

"No? Don't you go to a deaf school?"

Deaf school? No, he signed. *"Caterham High School. My school has ears that work."*

Say again.

Jake shrugged never mind. "A joke."

When she and Jake returned to the picnic with the two coolers, the sand castle contest was in full swing.

Without conversation they built their own, complete with moat and sand turrets and inlaid with small white beach stones. Amanda added a tiny

115

American flag and Jake brought two horseshoe crabs up from the water. *Monsters. Keep away strangers.*

"Gross."

At dinnertime the clambake was served with great fanfare. Jake and his father used pitchforks to lift off the seaweed and separate the food from the coals. Everybody clapped and cheered and then helped themselves to the Hacketts' feast.

Amanda stood back as the islanders and the rest of the Aldens helped themselves to lobsters, clams and mussels, corn and potatoes. She wasn't alone for long, however. While the rest of the group ate, Jake tugged her by the wrist, closer to the cooling pit.

Choose one thing. "Eat something!"

Before she could protest, he picked up two lobsters and pointed to the corner of his beach blanket. "Sit."

She did. Jake expertly cracked the claws of the lobster, then the tail, dipped the meat in melted butter, and fed her.

Jake was patient and funny. He had the most expressive face she'd ever seen. Half the time she had no idea what he was signing, but it gave her an excuse to watch him and look into his eyes, so she wouldn't let him stop. Sometimes, in the middle of a sentence, she'd recognize a gesture and repeat it. It was like charades, and when she understood, she felt like hugging him all over again. She knew he was pleased at the effort she was making, and that made her feel good, too.

By the time everyone had finished eating and

cleaning up, dusk had settled. While the adults gathered up their gear before dark, Jake handed out sparklers.

Amanda stood in the shadows and watched as Jake lit them for the children. Now the sand around her glittered in silvery brightness. The island was cooling off and she shivered, but the minute she rubbed her arms, Jake handed her his sweatshirt. She pulled it over her head and paused just long enough to fill her lungs with the same faint smell of charcoal and sea.

Jake watched her face bathed in the light of the sparklers. She was happy. She'd been happy all day and he sensed it in more than her words, more than her expressions.

Something startled her and she turned sharply around as the first of the Plymouth fireworks cascaded over them. He wanted to tell her he could remember the *Ka-boom* he knew she'd just heard. He wanted her to know that this was his favorite night on the island and he'd never shared it with anyone, except casually with the rest of the summer people.

His heart was full of what he kept inside. They both stood and looked at the distant shoreline, lit up by the explosions overhead. It's up to me, he told himself, and after a moment, he tugged her gently over to his blanket.

Amanda pulled her knees up and hugged them, the sweatshirt sleeves well over her fingers. She was warm where she pressed against his shoulder, and Jake wanted to put his arm around her. He wanted to walk her home in the dark and kiss her good night on the bluff. As he sat there, he imagined her throwing the ring out into the inky water. It would be the perfect ending to a perfect day. When he turned and watched her in the glow of the next display, she smiled at him. He knew encouragement when he saw it.

The fireworks were over too soon and too soon they were surrounded by her family. Dr. Alden led the way down to his end of the beach with his marine flashlight, and Jake walked with Amanda behind them in the dark.

He stopped at the bluff where the lawn of Pilgrim House began and the path veered off to his own house. "Good night," he said.

Great day, thank you, Amanda signed right under his nose so he could see.

Jake smiled and looked away. He thought for a moment, hedged, berated himself, and then, before he lost his nerve, he put his hands on her shoulders. He suddenly realized she was in the process of taking the ring from her pocket and putting it back on her finger, but he didn't let her go. Instead, he waited.

Her hands were raised. She hesitated and said something but it was too dark to lip read. She opened her fingers against his chest as if she might push him away, but he didn't give her the chance. Instead, he leaned closer and brushed his mouth over hers. Just like the first time, she kissed him back slowly and his heart leapt.

Amanda felt weightless, but before she could gather her thoughts, Jake let go. As suddenly as he'd kissed her, he turned and disappeared through the shadowed beach plum.

She stood by herself in the dark and listened to

the night sounds of the island. She watched the distant sweep of the lighthouse beam across the channel and then walked toward the dim lights of Pilgrim House, brushing Jake's sweatshirt sleeve against her cheek as she went.

Her half brothers were already upstairs, but her father called to her from the front parlor. Amanda stopped in the doorway and tilted her head as Dr. Alden grinned at his wife. They both had *the look*. They were up to something and they were about to spring it on her.

Dr. Alden stood up. "We have a surprise, Mandy. I know this hasn't been the best vacation so far. These past few days, you've seemed more down in the dumps than ever."

Nancy Alden broke in. "Frankly, I thought there'd be some friends for you when the summer houses opened."

"I guess I was pretty miserable till today," Amanda replied.

"We're giving you something to look forward to," her father continued. "We've arranged for you to have a guest for a week, here on the island."

Amanda tried to stay one step ahead of them. "A guest?"

"Chris is coming, a week from tomorrow."

It took a second to sink in. "Chris, here, next week?" She looked at her ring finger.

"It's all arranged. He's going to fly into Boston and take the limousine shuttle to Caterham. I'll teach you how to use the boat and you can even pick him up yourself, if you'd like. I called the Kings yesterday when we were in town."

Amanda looked at Jake's sweatshirt, but finally

put her arms around her father's neck and gave her stepmother a hug, too. "What a surprise."

"Then you're happy? I wasn't sure for a minute."

"Of course! It's wonderful. I can't wait."

It would be wonderful. It would be perfect, she'd make sure of it. After they'd talked over the details, Amanda went up to bed. She propped herself on her elbow and looked out her open window into the dark. No foghorn sounded, the night was littered with stars. If she craned her neck, she could see the edge of the bluff and the path to the Hacketts'. She could see the spot where she and Jake had kissed.

What would Chris think of all this if he knew? Amanda pressed her forehead and closed her eyes, afraid to admit what she felt for Jake, what she'd been feeling most of the day. In the dark, she twisted Chris's ring around on her finger. He'd be here in a week. She'd concentrate on that and it would make everything clear again. She'd show him every nook and cranny on the island, all the spots she'd written about. They'd picnic and swim and walk in the moonlight. It would be romantic, as romantic as this night had been.

She put her hand over her face and leaned back into the pillow, refusing to accept the confusion raging inside her. Nothing would spoil the week with Chris, nothing! As far as she was concerned, he couldn't get here fast enough. Then she could associate all the places she was growing to appreciate with the boy from home, the one who meant everything to her. She mustn't forget that Jake was her friend for the summer but Chris was forever.

Chapter 15

The following afternoon, Jake settled back against the flotation cushion in the cockpit of the Aldens' sloop. Amanda was beside him, wearing his sweatshirt and her pink bathing suit, with one hand on the tiller. He'd been sailing with her for more than an hour, drinking in the way she looked, the way she moved and smiled.

This was what his friends must feel; what he read in their faces when they talked about their girl-friends; what made them choose a date over hanging out with the guys. Being with Amanda chipped away at his loneliness. He couldn't put it in words, but it had to do with feeling separate, apart from

121

the world. It was as if being with her pulled him closer to everything he'd missed. Deafness was like swimming under water and Amanda Alden was there, on the surface.

Her closeness in the little boat, in the light of a sparkler, in his arms, was his link, and when she signed, when she understood him, two worlds merged. It made him feel like everybody else. She was talking and he turned to face her.

"No more kissing!" Amanda could tell by Jake's expression that he'd understood. Nevertheless, she touched her lips and cheek with her fingertips and shook her head. *No kiss.*

Jake laughed, which confused her. This was serious; it had to be discussed. Amanda had spent more than an hour with him, trying to figure out a way to bring up the events of the day and night before. She felt floppy inside, rattled. She knew plenty about boys, but none of it seemed to apply to Jake. He was an exception to every rule she knew.

The two of them were sailing the Aldens' boat, at Amanda's invitation. She'd sailed at camp for years, and besides horseback riding, she figured it was about the only other thing she could do on the island as well as Jake.

Originally she'd needed something comfortable, some place private, because she'd planned to talk to him. The trouble was, once they were off in the boat, she couldn't figure out how to bring up the subject. She joked instead, and joking lead to a dare, and now she was proving to Jake how well she could sail.

No wonder he laughed. She would, too, if he'd

brought up kissing in the middle of changing tacks across the channel. What a geek she was for blurting it out.

She groaned. "Jake, we have to talk about this." She held up her hand and displayed Chris's ring.

He made a tossing gesture with his hands toward the water.

"Right," she muttered. "Throw his ring overboard."

"I'm right," he replied, as he signed. *"You'll see."*

All she could see was that she was heading for trouble, but she also knew she was the happiest she'd been since the day she'd left Lockwood. Jake Hackett was awesome to look at and wonder about, a challenge to keep up with, mysterious, and just plain fun. Unless they were arguing, of course. Then the challenge disintegrated into frustration.

He was full of enough confidence to joke as he leaned next to her and started to use his hands again. *No kisses today. We'll hunt for horseshoe crabs.*

Amanda was lost. *Say again.*

"Horseshoe crabs. No kisses."

"Gross, and you know it."

Jake pretended to frown. *My kisses?*

"Jake you're impossible!" It felt good to tease and kid around. She hadn't thought he was the type, but she should have known by now that Jake wasn't any type, Jake was totally unique. She glanced down at Chris's ring, but instead of thinking about Chris, she thought about Jake going back to search for it, for her. Unconsciously she rubbed the sleeve of her sweatshirt and smiled.

Her daydreaming came to an end as Jake pointed off the wind and motioned for Amanda to tighten the sheet to adjust the sail.

"I know how to sail," she said.

She sat up on the coaming and motioned for Jake to move beside her. She yanked in the sheet until the sail was close hauled and the sloop was heeling over at its most efficient racing speed. Without asking, she took the tiller from Jake. "I'm going to show you a thing or two, Jake."

Not me!

You. "Understand?"

Oh, really, he said with his eyebrows, and held on as they sped across the narrow channel from the Pilgrim House bluff to the salt marsh shore of the barrier beach below the lighthouse. Back and forth, whooping and hollering, the two of them sailed, shifting from one side of the boat to the other in perfect synchronization. It had been a perfect demonstration of her seaworthy skills, but it came to a shuddering crunch of an ending as the little sloop stopped short.

Jake grabbed the boom as it swung precariously and Amanda peered over the side. They were in less than two feet of water. "We're aground!"

Jake slapped one hand against the other and pursed his lips.

She shook her finger. "Don't you even think about laughing. You knew all the time we were in shallow water. Jake Hackett — "

"You — sailor, remember?"

"Cute, Jake. Very cute."

He cocked his head and pointed to himself.

She blushed and mumbled, "Never mind," as they

tried to free themselves from the silty bottom.

Jake cooperated by moving to the same side of the boat as Amanda, but the sloop wouldn't budge. The water was clear enough for her to see that the shallows extended further than she'd thought. She was getting less sure of herself by the minute.

Next she tried pulling the sail back in and the centerboard up. They slid sideways toward the shore and stopped again. Jake did whatever she instructed but nothing made any difference.

They'd drifted just enough to be nosed well into the eel grass, which peaked up at the surface and ran from the shallows back to the marshy shoreline. Amanda didn't even want to think about what might be living there.

"You let this happen, do something," she cried as she yanked the boom across the cockpit.

You're the sailor.

Jake Hackett!

"Tide, Mayflower, trust the tide."

Amanda tried hard to understand him, but nothing was clear until he finger spelled: *T I D E.* They were an hour off high tide, which meant the water in the channel was still rising.

Lakes didn't have tides and shallows, she wanted to tell him. "How long?" she asked instead.

"Off in half an hour."

Like a balloon with a slow leak, Amanda sank back into the boat, slumped in defeat. Jake was already undoing the lines from their turnbuckles and pulling down the mainsail. "Half an hour to wait," he said. *Half an hour.*

"I'll practice signing till then."

"How about kissing?"

125

Jake! She shook her head and touched her fingertips to her lips and cheek: *No kiss.* Then she
grinned at him. "I don't need to practice."

Yes, you do. He was blushing furiously.

Amanda touched his cheek. "I need to be serious.
You and I need to talk about things."

I'm deaf.

"No jokes!"

Jake knew very well what Amanda was struggling
to say. Didn't she know that her face was as expressive as her words? He didn't want to watch her
tell him the kisses had been a mistake, that yesterday shouldn't have happened.

Impulsively, he got out of the boat and motioned
for her to follow. Careful not to step on the delicate
eel grass, Jake walked from the grounded boat,
through the shin-deep shallows, to shore. When she
caught up with him, he was studying the estuary in
the salt marsh.

There were horseshoe crabs, of course, but also
snails and tiny crabs. Sandpipers skittered around
the grasses. Jake motioned to Amanda. *Sit down.
No talk.*

Jake, please, Amanda protested, but she also sat
down.

When she was next to him on the sand, his pulse
settled down, closer to normal. She was studying a
tern as it dive-bombed the shallows in search of
lunch.

To fill the silence, Jake found a periwinkle snail
and placed it on his open palm. He put his other
hand against his throat so he could feel his vocal
chords vibrate, and then he hummed. Slowly the

126

snail oozed its way out of the tiny shell. Amanda was as wide-eyed as he'd expected.

"How?"

He shrugged and gently eased the little creature into her palm. Amanda tried, self-consciously, and the trick of nature worked for her, too. He thought about telling her that as a child it was one of the ways he could prove to himself that he still made noise.

Instead, he studied the shore and picked up a piece of sea glass, which he turned over in his palm. Amanda was a lot like it, he thought. Those first days she'd been all sharp and jagged, too glittery, but time on the island was wearing away her sharp edges. She was softer, prettier, more approachable. Mayflower made him dare to dream, not just of moments, but of whole days like yesterday, of a future time when he wouldn't feel separate and apart.

They sat and watched for long, comfortable minutes until she finger spelled *K* and tapped her shoulder and waist: *King*.

"Chris King is coming here next week."

The mood vanished. *Island?*

Yes.

Jake was thoughtful. *He'll hate it here, Mayflower. He'll be just like you, first week here.*

Friends, Jake? She signed hesitantly.

Friends, Mayflower. What choice did he have?

They got up together and walked back to the sloop, which was shifting in the rising tide. During the return sail, Amanda tried to return his sweatshirt.

You wear Chris's ring, my sweatshirt, he signed.

Once back on shore, Jake went home to exercise

127

Lightning and tend the garden. He left after elaborately shaking hands good-bye. His expression stayed serious only as long as hers did. The minute Amanda laughed, Jake laughed, too.

That afternoon, Amanda went back on the water with her father for a lesson in operating the Whaler. "You'll really let me take this across the bay by myself?"

"If you pass muster."

He had her call the harbormaster and radio that they were coming into Caterham harbor, and then gave her the chance to maneuver the outboard across the channel to the mainland. "I'll make you an islander yet," Dr. Alden laughed. "Or else Jake will."

It was hard to talk over the roar of the engine, but she shouted, "Do you like Jake?"

"Yes. He's good for you, Mandy. Teaches you about the island."

"I hope Chris likes him," she shouted back.

Dr. Alden raised his eyebrows in reply.

It seemed terribly important that Chris like Jake. They could certainly pal around together part of the week. Couldn't they? They could all be friends, buddies. . . . Amanda sighed at her own wishful thinking. What she needed were the girls in Lockwood. Her friends at home would understand the difference between a boyfriend and a friend who happened to be a boy. They knew about predicaments like the one she was in.

Chapter
16

Two days before Chris's arrival, Dr. Alden agreed that Amanda knew enough about the Whaler to try a run across the bay into Caterham. With her father's approval, Amanda convinced Jake that he would be just the person to accompany her before she made her solo trip to pick up her boyfriend.

Thursday morning was cool and Amanda wore Jake's sweatshirt over her shirt and stonewashed skirt. She had a list of errands and a load of dirty clothes for the laundromat. Independence flooded through her as her father waved her off and she nosed the motorboat out into deep water and around the island to the Hacketts' dock.

Amanda was early, so she docked the boat and went up the bluff for Jake, intending to show him how well she'd secured the mooring lines without help. He was in the kitchen, going over a grocery list with his mother.

Amanda stayed long enough to make small talk with Mrs. Hackett and watch her sign last-minute instructions to Jake. The three of them walked as far as the vegetable garden, where Jake's mother stopped and said good-bye. She snapped her fingers, as if remembering something, as she noticed Amanda's left hand.

"I'm glad to see that Jake finally gave you your ring. It sat on his dresser for days."

"For days?" Amanda asked.

Mrs. Hackett nodded. "He kept telling me he didn't know who it belonged to, but I remembered seeing it on your hand the day you came over with your little brothers. I pestered Jake to ask you about it, so I'm glad to see he finally did."

Jake had said he didn't know who it belonged to? Amanda looked down at her hand, as if there'd been a mistake. She managed to make a harmless comment to Mrs. Hackett, but she didn't dare look at Jake as she tried to make sense of the conversation. "*You* told Jake it might be mine?"

"Yes. I found it in the pocket of his jeans when I took them off the line. It could have fallen back into the grass and gotten lost all over again. I'm glad it's back on your finger. Must belong to somebody special."

Amanda nodded, and Jake's mother finished and waved them off.

* * *

Jake caught the gist of the conversation and he fought dread as Amanda walked beside him to the boat. He'd never explained the ring to his mother because she would have asked all about Amanda and her boyfriend. She would have fussed over his hurt feelings and made an issue of a thousand other things he didn't want to discuss.

He'd meant to tell Amanda the truth on one of their walks or rides or sails. He'd had millions of opportunities, but he wasn't good at that kind of thing. Amanda had been so grateful and thought he was so wonderful, and by then it was too late. Mayflower had given him the role of hero and he liked it. All these days together and he hadn't even kissed her for fear of rocking the precarious boat they were in. How was he supposed to confess, then make her understand emotions he barely understood himself?

When they reached the wildflowers, three angry taps hit his shoulder. His face burned as he looked at Amanda.

Why, was all she signed.

Accident. I was going to tell you.

"Tell me! Jake, did you have the ring before I borrowed the waders the second time?"

Mayflower —

"Did you?"

He nodded.

"That means you had the ring before I went back into that muck that afternoon. You let me go back and work and work — and cry! You knew how desperate I was. You knew how I felt. You knew how important this ring is. You knew everything! How could you pretend you didn't know

131

it was mine? How could you be so mean?"

It didn't matter that he missed half of what she said. Her expression said everything.

Amanda signed, *kiss*. "You let me kiss you and throw my arms around you. I thought you were a hero, that you went back and looked on purpose." *Stupid girl. Stupid, stupid, girl*, was the way she finished.

Jake grabbed her hands. *No, you're not. My fault, Mayflower.* There was so much he wanted to tell her, but he knew it would drive her away. He didn't know what to do with himself. Amanda Alden was like the wind against his cheek, always making her presence felt even when she wasn't there.

How could he tell her the hated ring was a constant reminder of the real world she came from, and the boy he couldn't compete with. She could never understand the risks he took when he opened up to her. There was no way to explain that when he kept the ring from her, it gave him control. It put her in his world and made her dependent on him, even when he hated himself for doing it.

She yanked her hands back, and Amanda got into the boat in stormy silence. She glared at Jake who stood beside her on the pier. "Don't back out now. I need you, since I can't get Chris by myself. But I'm still ripped at you, Jake." She bent her fingers and signed, *Grouch*.

He knew she meant *angry*, but it was the wrong time to correct her.

The only good thing about the next twenty minutes was the ride. Amanda was confident at the wheel and handled the boat fine in the calm waters. When they reached the harbor at the mainland, she maneuvered through the boats in the Caterham anchorage, and then indicated that she needed help guiding the Whaler into the basin. Her expression told Jake clearly that she hated to ask him, hated depending on him, but that was why he was along.

Once they were docked, Jake picked up the Aldens' laundry bag without being asked, and watched as Amanda expertly cleated the mooring lines of the Whaler to the slip. When she caught his eye, he couldn't help but smile a little. It was a far cry from her first attempt with the Hacketts' nautical line, the day she rode to the island on the *Sharon*. Jake could tell by her expression that, as usual, they both knew what the other was thinking.

Jake slung the laundry up onto the truckbed and waited for Amanda to get into the cab. Even hosed down, the truck smelled of fish and sea bottom, and the space between them was littered with odds and ends associated with lobstering. The ride from the landing into the main streets was thankfully short and Jake parked in front of the laundromat. This time Amanda insisted on carrying the load herself.

"Errands at the marine shop." Jake said.

Amanda pointed to the grocery store.

Half an hour.

Me, too.

They separated and Jake hoped that in those thirty minutes, he could compose a way to explain why he'd kept the ring. Mayflower's boyfriend would be on the island soon and then Jake would lose his chance. Whatever he and Mayflower shared would disappear with the arrival of Christopher King. It was Jake's biggest fear.

He picked up an engine part for his father as well

133

as the mail and was back at the laundromat ahead of time. Since his family did their island laundry at their own house in Caterham, it was one of the few places in town he'd never been in.

It wasn't air-conditioned and the old place was steamy. It smelled of bleach and soap and, although Jake couldn't hear the machines, the small red lights told him which were in operation. The place was empty, with the exception of a heavyset woman at the end of the room, reading a movie magazine.

Jake walked down the row to the dryer, which had the Aldens' laundry bag on the floor in front of it. His head ached with all the conversation, frustration, and anger inside him. He didn't want to be in Caterham, in the hearing world.

Maybe he'd have a chance to explain if they went aground again, if Amanda were stuck with him in the salt marsh, or if they were out in the cemetery. Sometimes his deafness felt like drowning. He could save himself if he knew what words to use, if he dared put his feelings into sign. If they were alone together, Amanda might figure it all out herself, but not here, never here.

Jake opened the dryer and lifted the finished load from inside into his arms. Suddenly he caught a flash of movement in his side vision as a sharp pain seared the back of his neck. Jake spun around in shock. The woman had rolled her magazine into a bat and was about to hit him again.

The pain shocked Jake into action. He dropped the clothes and raised his arm to deflect the second *thawck* as confusion and outrage tore through him. The woman's face was crimson and distorted with anger. Jake stepped back. As he tried to make sense of what she was doing, she only got angrier.

Amanda had heard the high-pitched woman's voice even over the squeak of the old screen door as she'd entered the laundromat. "Don't you ignore me," the manager yelled from the back of the room. "You got no ticket for that laundry."

Amanda froze with her hand still on the door as the woman lumbered up behind Jake. "What are you, deaf? I'm talkin' to you. You punk kids think you can come in here and fool around with other people's laundry. It ain't funny and don't you ignore me." When Jake didn't respond, she rolled her magazine and swatted him.

"Hey," Amanda called out from the front, but it was too late. Jake winced in surprise and wheeled around. The woman kept scolding and Jake finally began to speak. As he tried to explain, the manager recoiled from him with a look on her face that was part horror and part disgust.

It was the first time in weeks that Amanda had thought about how Jake sounded to other people, and she felt as though she'd been punched in the stomach. She ran between the row of machines and reached Jake as he spoke again.

"He's deaf, for heaven's sake. He didn't hear you and he was only taking out *my* laundry," Amanda cried as she fished her ticket stub from her pocket.

The woman's complexion mottled in embarrassment. She didn't look at Jake but spoke directly to Amanda. "Well, can't he read? Don't he know the rules?"

She pointed angrily to the posted sign on the far wall, which stated clearly that no laundry could be shifted without a ticket. "We get kids in here all the time, messing around just for kicks. How was I to know? Why don't he wear a hearing aid? If he ain't normal, then he don't belong in here."

Jake spoke anyway. "I didn't see the sign. I didn't know about the ticket."

The woman looked as though she'd tasted lemon rind as she kept her eyes on Amanda. "What'd he say?"

Humiliation ran through Jake like an electric shock. "I said I didn't know about the ticket."

Amanda grabbed his arm. "I'll take care of this," she told him as she raised her hands. Instead of speaking, she signed. *Jake is deaf but you are a stupid, grouchy woman. Stupid, grouchy woman*, she repeated.

Before she'd finished, Jake strode out and left both of them. Although the truck was just down the block, the walk seemed endless. He got into the cab and gripped the steering wheel. Silently he damned the world, the town, and the girl who'd brought him over to it.

The engine was already running, and he had his hand on the gearshift by the time Amanda threw the laundry bag into the back and climbed into the cab.

She circled her heart.

Without comment, Jake ground the gears into reverse and drove back to the landing.

Episodes like this had happened before and he knew they would happen again, but none of that eased the pain gnawing at him. Maybe he could have sluffed it off, chalked it up to ignorant people if Amanda hadn't been there. It was her fault, her laundry . . . her idea . . . her world. To make it worse, she'd taken over as if he were helpless.

136

The tentative touch of her fingers on his shoulder made him turn. He parked the truck and put all the anger into sign. *Do your own laundry, take care of your own things, and let me take care of mine! Don't sign for me! I was there. I would have made her understand. I can take care of myself. Not you! I don't need you to speak for me.*

He ignored her hurt expression and puzzlement as she tried to follow his hands. Jake got out and stayed silent all the way back across the bay. Amanda was at the wheel of the Whaler, so caught up in replaying the nightmare that she barely paid attention to what she was doing. Once they were safely at the Hackett dock, she tried to talk to him again.

I'm sorry, Jake.

Your world, not mine.

Not true, she countered. "I know how you must feel. I know how hurt and embarrassed you are. When you talk, you sound okay to me, Jake. I understand you. Don't worry about other people."

Other people! That said it all. *"Other people, different world. Your world, your ring, your King."*

In his anger and humiliation, it was all related, all spun together like a net that kept him under water, floundering. He wanted nothing but to be back in his own place.

"It doesn't matter. Don't get so upset," Amanda tried lamely. She watched him tap his shoulder and hip and recognized the sign for King, the one she'd made up for Chris.

"This doesn't have anything to do with Chris."

"Everything to do with Chris," Jake replied. *Your world, his world.*

"It was a mistake at the laundromat. She was a stupid, mean woman. Aren't any deaf people wrong sometimes? You kept my ring, Jake! Wasn't that stupid and mean?"

You won't ever understand.

"I want to."

You can't because you're not deaf. Jake's dark eyes flashed and he got out of the Whaler.

Say again.

No.

Impulsively, Amanda pulled off Jake's sweatshirt and threw it to him. He caught it, turned, and marched up his pier.

Chapter
17

For the rest of the day, part of Amanda hurt for Jake and part of her was still hurt for herself. Her heart went out to him when she thought about the laundromat. But just as quickly it frosted over when she thought about his resentment of her help, not to mention letting her grovel around in the mud when he'd had the ring right in his pocket. Being a friend of Jake's was like trying to sail in erratic wind: smooth one minute, out of control the next.

For the first time since the Fourth of July, Amanda was grateful that she hadn't gotten more involved with him. She didn't have the energy or the time to dwell on any of it. Chris was coming to the island

and for a whole week she could concentrate on the boy who really mattered.

Nothing helped. Jake covered every inch of the island woods with Lightning, following paths he hadn't taken in years, out to his boyhood hideouts, through the tangled overgrowth of a farmstead washed away during the 1938 hurricane. He hardly paid attention because his brain was too busy focusing on the shambles his life was in.

Anger spilled out of him. Nothing felt the same without Amanda. Couldn't she have figured out that it hurt to be used for her trial run across the channel? It hurt to think she'd practiced with him so she could pick up Chris. If he hadn't gone, the incident in the laundromat would never have happened and then she wouldn't have felt the need to defend him.

How could he have left himself so open? How could one small blonde girl be part of every lousy thing that had happened to him, and every good thing, too? Why hadn't he had the brains to see that his dreams were beyond his reach? For the first time since he was a kid, tears welled up in his eyes. He leaned over and buried his face in Lightning's mane.

In Caterham the airport shuttle discharged passengers at the post office and, by chance, Jake saw Christopher King before Amanda did. The afternoon of Chris's arrival, Jake was in the fish market's alley. As he slid the last bin of lobsters across the truckbed to his father, the stretch limousine from Logan Airport stopped.

Jake shaded his eyes as it pulled away down the main street, leaving a tall blond boy alone at the sidewalk bench. The guy looked athletic and rich, just the way Jake had imagined him. His clothes and hair were conservative rather than stylish. He glanced around, then checked his watch as he put down his luggage. He probably smelled of after-shave or hair mousse. He didn't look like the type who would understand how a girl could lose his ring in mud flats, digging for clams.

The guy caught sight of the usual crowd at the sailboard shop and Jake watched him as he eyed a group of the female instructors, just back from the beach. Eventually one of them waved and started across the street toward him.

Anger simmered in Jake. This was the kid Amanda was devoted to? What did he care? Mayflower could take care of herself just fine. Looking across the alley at Christopher King made Jake feel terrible. Jealousy and guilt were a crummy combination.

Both boys glanced around for Amanda, and Jake fought the urge to go to the landing, in case she was having trouble with the boat. She was late and her boyfriend was getting impatient. Jake had a hard time envisioning Chris waiting for any girl.

It she was in trouble, Mack Howland, the har-bormaster, would help. Besides, Jake told himself, Amanda wasn't any of his business now. He'd have about as much success competing with Christopher King as a seagull against a hurricane.

The guy was still standing alone when Jake and his father left to pick up their bait. However, an hour later, when the Hacketts drove back down the street and returned to the town landing, he was gone.

* * *

Since the post office was just around the corner from the landing, Amanda hurried by foot around to Water Street. Chris was already there, on the bench, talking with a girl in a Windsurfer T-shirt. Amanda was breathless by the time she reached him.

"Oh, I'm so glad you're here," she cried, as the sailboarder went back across the street.

"I've been here for half an hour," Chris muttered as he hugged her. "At least I scratched up some company."

Amanda explained about the crowded harbor and her first solo use of the boat. She was a little hurt by his lack of understanding, but he'd had a long flight, then the bus, and then the wait. What could she expect?

He looked as cute as always, and he had on the green polo shirt she thought made his eyes so blue. "I've missed you," she whispered.

"Mandy, I thought you'd forgotten me. You don't even have a phone out there, so I couldn't call or anything," Chris added.

Amanda mussed his hair. "I wouldn't forget you! It just took me longer in the boat. Oh, Chris, there's so much I want to show you. It's so wonderful on the island, so quiet and beautiful. I'm glad we don't have a phone."

He picked up his monogrammed duffel bag. "Yeah, well, I'm not much of a writer. We'd do better if we could call each other, like normal people."

Amanda bristled. "Not all *normal* people can speak on the phone."

"What's that supposed to mean?"

She waved it off. "Never mind. This way I get love letters. You can't reread a phone call, Chris." She wished his short notes were more like love letters. He rarely mentioned anything but the guys and the parties in Lockwood.

"Where'd you park?" he asked as Amanda started off.

"We're on foot. It's just a few blocks around to the water and the boat."

"We have to walk?"

"You'll get used to it!"

Chris gave her a puzzled look. "You didn't use to be this bossy."

Amanda grinned. "I haven't had anybody else to depend on but myself. Maybe I've changed."

As she walked with him through Caterham, Amanda pointed out the shops and talked about her day trips. At the fish market she automatically looked down the alley to the empty loading platform. "That's where the Hacketts — the family I wrote about — bring their lobsters."

"The family with the deaf kid," Chris added.

"Jake. Yes, Jake's deaf." It took a moment, but Amanda smiled at Chris. "Oh, there's so much to tell! I've been learning to sign. Watch." She formed *K* with her right hand and tapped her shoulder and opposite hip. *King*. "That's your sign. It means your name. I'm Mayflower." She showed him and added the ones for her brothers.

"Try it," she said as they rounded the corner and entered the town landing.

"No way, Mandy." Chris looked around.

Amanda hugged his arm as they walked. "Don't be so self-conscious."

"Then don't ask me to act like a geek."

Amanda was about to answer him, but she let it

143

pass and cheered up when Chris got enthusiastic about the Whaler.

"All right!" he exclaimed as they got aboard. "We can have some fun in this!"

Against her better judgment, she put it in full throttle as they cleared the anchorage and sped across the channel in record time. Chris's happiness made her happy. He laughed and whooped it up, but the roar of the outboard engine made it impossible to do more than shout short messages.

She pointed to the Hacketts'. "That's Jake's farm," she shouted. "At low tide, there's good clamming out here."

"What?"

"Low tide. Clams."

"Yuk."

"I had lobster on the Fourth of July. It was great."

"What?"

Amanda got her hands moving. *Lobster. Fourth of July.* When she finished signing, she cut the engine down to headway speed and meandered along the shoreline.

"What the heck was that," Chris asked, no longer having to shout quite as loudly.

"The sign for lobsters. I said I ate lobster on the Fourth of July. It was the first one I'd ever had." She could feel Chris study her curiously as they continued around the island.

"Pretty lousy beach," he said.

"I used to think so, too. It's rocky, but there are smooth parts."

"Does it always smell like this?"

"What?"

Chris held his nose.

"Tide's going out. That's the mud flats."

"Yuk."

"You'll get used to it." Amanda didn't speak again until she'd docked the boat in front of Pilgrim House and turned off the engine. "That's better! I'm so glad you're here, Chris." Again, she hugged him.

Chris held her long enough to kiss her. "It's all for you, Mandy. You wouldn't catch me in a place this dead unless I had a darn good reason."

She laughed. "I'll turn you into a Yankee island lover, you'll see. Just give it a chance. If you're not too tired, let's go put your stuff away and we can take a walk. There're so many out of the way — "

"Walk? You really like all this walking?" He grabbed his duffel bag and shook his head.

"I'm sure I told you there weren't any cars." Amanda led him cheerfully over the stony shore and up to the house, trying not to let his lack of enthusiasm hurt.

"You might have. I guess that was in one of your first letters." He was looking over the island as if she'd been teasing and any minute an automobile would appear on a paved roadway.

Amanda didn't like the tone of his voice any more than his words. She hadn't spoken this much to a boy in weeks, she hadn't needed to. "Try to understand, Chris. I felt just like you do when we first got here, but it's not so bad, really. A lot of Clark's Island is wonderful. You'll see, I promise."

They crossed the lawn together and Amanda looked at him for a sign of encouragement. Suddenly she saw herself through Jake's eyes and the realization embarrassed her. That was the way she'd acted with him, insulting a lot of what he loved most in the world.

"I sure hope so," Chris was muttering.

Amanda forced herself to pay attention. Maybe teasing would help. She pointed toward the small, narrow building off by itself. "You even get to use a real outhouse."

He blanched. "You're kidding. You mean I've got to go in that thing? No way did you mention *that* in any letter! Geeze, Amanda, what's next?"

Amanda shrugged. "Next we write home and tell your mother to send up your sense of humor. You forgot it."

Chapter 18

Déjà vu swept over Jake as he saddled Lightning. The sun had dipped behind the Standish Monument, across the harbor. He wanted to ride at dusk and work out the soreness in his forearms from hours of banding lobster claws. He wanted to clear his head from a day of smelling bait and scrubbing waders.

Maybe Mayflower and her boyfriend were walking the beach, hand-in-hand. What if they were in the field, or up on the rock? Once again he felt like a prisoner on his own island, afraid of venturing out for fear of who he might run into. Once again, he railed at himself and signed, *Stupid*. Whose island was it, anyway?

By the time Amanda and Chris reached the path into the field, Amanda was half hoping they might run into Jake. It would give her a chance to change the subject. Chris hadn't talked about anything but himself, her friend Heather Taylor, and Lockwood parties since they'd finished dinner. Heather's name came up so often, Amanda wondered if she should worry. As they passed the wild canes, she pointed out the raspberries and popped a few into Chris's mouth so he'd stop raving about the band at his Fourth of July, country club dance.

"I went to my first clambake," Amanda said. "You should see how they cook it all, right in the sand with hot coals and water to make steam over the seaweed."

"Seaweed?"

"Yup. Everything is steamed in seaweed. Delicious. And the best fireworks . . . We watched right from the beach."

"Somebody's out there on a horse," Chris said, barely interested.

Nerves fluttered in Amanda's stomach. "That'll be Jake."

"The deaf kid?"

Instead of answering, Amanda walked under the tunnel of leaves and out into the opening. Lightning snorted from the middle of the field. It was the first she'd seen Jake since their awful excursion, and she had no idea what to expect.

Jake's response didn't help. He stayed on the horse and looked at her with his usual wary expression. His brown eyes were serious, guarded, and although the reins were loose in his hands, Amanda could tell he was as tense as she. He wore only jeans and old boating shoes, and looked as much a part of that meadow as the granite rock behind him. Amanda fooled with her hair, as self-conscious as her first day on the island. She forced herself to wave him over.

Chris looked confused. "Wait a minute, that's Jake? He's our age! I thought he was a kid, like your brothers. You never said he looked like that."

"Like what?"

"Oh, come on, Mandy!" Chris mumbled. He looked from her back to Jake. "Forget it."

The moment stretched uncomfortably. Amanda caught Jake's eye and signed to him, then lectured herself on being cheerful. Jake looked as though he was doing the same thing.

"What the heck are you saying," Chris whispered.

"You don't have to whisper, silly. I'm introducing you."

Jake got down from the horse and the boys shook hands as Amanda nudged Chris. "Say something."

"Why? He can't hear me."

Jake dropped his hand.

"I'm sorry," she told both of them. "Chris, talk to Jake, not to me. He can read your lips." This wasn't going the way she'd planned.

"Hi, Jake," Chris replied.

Hello, Jake signed.

Amanda knew he wouldn't speak. After the incident in the laundromat, she doubted that she'd ever hear his voice again.

As the three of them stood together, Chris slung

his arm around Amanda's shoulder. "Great meeting you, Jake. Mandy, I didn't come all this way to watch a guy ride a horse," he said.

Amanda was as conscious of the weight of Chris's arm as she was of Jake's expression. "We have to go, Jake. I just wanted you two to meet."

Jake seemed relieved as he got back up on Lightning, and without looking back, he nudged the mare back across the field.

Amanda and Chris went back down their own path. "Not real sociable," Chris said.

"Were you?" she snapped.

"How'd you expect me to act? I don't know any sign language."

"You don't have to. You just have to act normal."

Chris stopped on the grass. "Mandy, are you telling me off because I didn't carry on some dumb conversation with a guy I don't know? We shook hands. What more do you want? What's with you, anyway?"

"Me?" Amanda caught herself. Nothing felt right inside, but it wasn't Chris's fault, and if she didn't watch out she'd ruin everything they had together. She sighed and leaned against him, and the minute Chris put his arm back around her, she apologized.

The night dragged. Under the brittle brightness of the living room gaslights, Jake tried to concentrate on a book. His father shuffled bills at the desk in the corner and massaged the furrow between his eyebrows with his index finger.

Next to him, Sharon Hackett sat in a straight-back chair, making lobster trap nets. She could fashion a new net as easily as someone else might crochet a doily.

There was a moon. The same one that had shone on Jake as he'd walked Amanda home after the fireworks now dappled the beach and the bluff and every other place he imagined her to be. What Jake imagined made concentrating on his book impossible.

His sweatshirt that she'd worn lay beside him on the couch but he couldn't bring himself to put it on. The charcoal residue was gone, and in its place the fleece smelled of soap and a cologne Jake had never noticed on Amanda until he'd kissed her.

Jake had read somewhere that the things people fear were the things beyond their control. His father had a healthy respect for the vagaries of the sea, but his fear was of the pollution of his waters, the constant threat to his way of life.

Jake had seen his mother afraid, when the boat was overdue or his father took chances with the weather. "I wish love were enough to keep him safe," she was always saying.

Love, fear . . . Jake was prickly with them, but he wouldn't name the feelings, not when they stemmed from a girl and the changes she'd brought with her. Abruptly, he got up, unaware of the noise he made or the sudden glances from his parents. The screen door squeaked, then slammed behind him as he went out into the night.

The walk at sunrise had not gone over very well. Amanda tried not to blame Chris. He was still tired, the island was unfamiliar, and his idea of beauty wasn't a departing lobster boat. He'd made the effort to get up and take the walk, but he mentioned more than once that he was doing it for her, as if it were a major sacrifice. She should have known better. There were plenty of other "normal" things to do, things that wouldn't make him as cranky.

As the visit continued, however, it got harder to hide her disappointment in Chris's attitude. After two days, she was hard-pressed to come up with anything he enjoyed except listening to his tapes on the boom box and cruising in the Whaler.

She loved the way he looked and the way he dressed; she wanted him as perfect on the inside as he was on the outside. They'd never argued much before, not in Lockwood, where they had everything in common and friends around them. She didn't want to start now; she wanted Chris to be happy. The solution finally came in the form of a simple suggestion from Dr. Alden. "Why don't you two get off the island?"

Southern Massachusetts baked in a typical July heatwave. It made the weather as volatile as Jake's disposition. By midweek, as the beaches loaded with sunbathers, the horizon filled with billowing clouds, which shaped and reshaped under the prevailing winds. They were beautiful to watch as they caught the light or trapped the sun.

At first light, when the Hacketts went to work, some were soft and cotton-candy pink. Some were gray as oyster shells and full of thunder, but it never rained. The clouds dissipated as the *Sharon* worked her way out and back, leaving the island parched and the sun worshippers to their tans.

Now, Jake looked at the wisps that were left on the horizon as he put the last of the clams in his six-quart basket and stood up straight. Well out in the channel, the all-too-familiar silhouette of a Whaler skimmed past. The sun burned his bare shoulders and his mood was as black as the sea mud that had dried on his forearms. He itched on the outside and ached on the inside. Even Lightning got on his nerves.

The Alden boys had spotted Jake one afternoon and had stayed long enough to display their gifts. Chris had bought Eric a new beach ball from the souvenir stand at the public barrier beach and Todd a T-shirt from the Caterham General Store. From then on, no matter how hard he tried not to, Jake noted daily the absence of the Alden motorboat.

He clomped through the silt and up to the shore. What did he care where Amanda went? She and her boyfriend were both the type for public beaches, radios, wall-to-wall kids, and boat parties. He could do that, too, if he wanted, anytime at all.

Amanda sat up and rubbed sunblock on Chris's shoulders. He had on new Hawaiian-print jams they'd bought together at the sailboard shop. They complemented her pink two-piece bathing suit.

As much as she liked rock music, the blare from a neighboring boom box was competing with the station Chris had found on his, giving her a headache. "I don't suppose we could find a spot by ourselves and just listen to seagulls or watch the clouds for a while," she quipped.

"You've been on that island too long. The lack of electricity's gone to your head, Mandy. What's summer without music and crowds to hang out with?" Chris tickled her and ogled a college girl walking past in a bikini.

"I'm serious!"

"About me, I hope."

As usual, Amanda kept her thoughts to herself. In their days together she'd discovered lots of things about Chris she'd never noticed in Lockwood. One of them was that he never wanted to be serious about much of anything.

Above her the sky was an incredible shade of blue, punctuated by white-gray clouds. It was the kind of thing she wished Chris would notice on his own. From the boat she'd tried to point out things like floating lobster buoys, which dotted the bay, or the estuary where she'd run aground, but he'd change the subject or kiss her instead of listening. Chris King was a lousy listener.

Amanda looked at him as he watched some girls in a nearby volleyball game. Didn't he know that his interest in other girls hurt? It bothered her when he referred to Heather Taylor, back in Lockwood, couldn't he see that? Instead of discussing it, she rolled over and let the sand play through her fingers.

It was nearly three o'clock and she wondered if the *Sharon* had returned to the island. She wondered if Jake was out in his drying yard, yanking off his work boots. Had he watched these clouds as he pulled his lobster pots?

Amanda got to her feet. "I'm going for a walk, Chris. You can come along if you want to."

Chapter
19

Jake stopped counting the days of Chris King's visit well before the week was out. Mayflower and her boyfriend belonged to the world off island. Maybe he would, too, someday, maybe not. All he knew for certain was that as the days inched along without Amanda, life started to feel the way it used to. He refused to think about whether that felt good or bad; in fact, he tried not to feel anything.

He hadn't walked on the beach in days because it gave him too much to think about. However, since his serenity was returning, he swam after dinner and headed for the deserted end, which had no associations for him. The stretch was strewn with rocks, undergrowth, nesting gulls, and their droppings. It didn't appeal to him much, but it was the one place he was sure to be left alone.

The sun was still a few hours from setting, but the heat no longer shimmered on the rocks. Jake skipped a stone into the bay and watched a catboat under sail as he walked. He hadn't gone more than fifty yards around the bend, into the scrub that hung over the water, when he spotted Amanda and Chris.

He was angry immediately at the intrusion, but he stood still until everything inside him felt normal and then walked up to them. They were arguing, and when Chris pointed at him, Amanda turned.

She was crouched on the rocks with her hands open over a seagull, and Chris was shaking his head. Jake forced himself not to react as Chris bent down and put his arm around Amanda and told her what to say to him.

Jake had already lip read perfectly: "There's your deaf friend. He knows about this stuff, too bad he can't hear. Somebody should talk some sense into you. I'm telling you, Mandy, you'll get all attached to it and it'll die. It'll break your heart, I know you."

Jake clenched his jaw and looked Amanda in the eye as she turned away from Chris.

"Jake! This poor gull is injured. I know I can nurse it back to health. You can tell us what to do. Help Chris understand."

This was the girl who couldn't stand horseshoe crabs? There were better ways to show off newfound nature skills than rescuing half-dead seagulls.

Jake made a face. *Stupid idea. King is right, the gull will die. Die, Mayflower. Stupid.* He made it simple, and when her eyes widened in surprise, he knew she'd understood.

"Jake!"

Dead bird. Disease.

"What'd he say?" Chris asked Amanda.

"I don't know exactly, but he agrees with you."
Even though she muttered, Jake understood.

"Thanks a lot, Jake," Amanda said.

It didn't take hearing for Jake to pick up the sarcasm. He watched as she hugged the flopping bird and lead the way into the undergrowth toward Pilgrim House.

The last Jake saw of them together was the next morning. He was in his own motorboat, checking traps near the shore, and the Whaler passed him. Chris was at the wheel with his arm around Amanda and they waved as they headed across the channel into Caterham.

At fifteen, Amanda's life had been laid out in front of her in black and white. What others chose for her had pretty much been okay. She went to a private school because her father sent her there; she'd gone to camp because her mother had. She wore the kind of clothes her friends did and only dated guys from the right crowd because it was her crowd. More than anything, she wanted to love Christopher King. Everybody else did and she had the same taste, the same crushes as her friends.

After breakfast, the third Sunday in July, one week after his arrival, Amanda kissed Chris good-bye in front of the Caterham Post Office. With tears in her eyes, she watched the limousine pull away, taking him back to the airport and home to Lockwood.

She got back to Clark's Island with a whole hot, empty day to face. Her father and stepmother understood her mood and took the boys sailing to give her time alone. She was too miserable to thank them.

Amanda changed into her old blue maillot bathing suit and left Pilgrim House to check on the gull. She'd named it Sandy and kept it in a box behind the outhouse. It wasn't faring much better than either boy had said it would, but it was eating and not flopping around as much. She was determined to nurse it back to health to prove her point.

The parched grass broke under her bare feet and the stubble prickled as she walked across the side yard. The box was tipped on its side and empty. Amanda turned around, feeling as she had the day her brothers disappeared, weeks earlier. She looked for the bird along the bordering undergrowth and went into the woods as far as the cemetery.

"Sandy?" she called in a low voice. "Poor little gull, where are you?"

Jake kicked a derelict soda can all the way from his beach to the tip of the island. The tide was out and he walked the exposed bed gingerly, avoiding barnacled rocks. He watched pea-sized bubbles pop the silt, indicating clam beds, but he'd harvested his week's limit.

The minute he rounded the bend, he spotted the bevy of gulls in the air over the rocks and knew something had disturbed them. Amanda was back above the high-water mark, bent over the rough shoreline with a garden trowel.

He wasn't surprised or angry. She was wearing the same bathing suit she'd worn the first time he'd seen her. Jake hated the fact that he remembered that, but there wasn't much about her he'd been able to forget.

He moved to the ledge of rock above her as she buried the gull. When she sensed she was being watched, she turned her head, and only then could he tell how miserable she was. They looked at each other but he ignored the urge to go to her. Instead, he leaned back on his elbows and studied the clouds, puffing and reforming like yeasted dough.

When the gull was buried, she stood up and dusted herself off. Jake didn't stir, which forced the next move on her. From the corner of his eye, he caught Amanda's departure up into the path. Unconsciously, he let out the breath he hadn't realized he'd been holding, and refused to acknowledge his disappointment.

The clouds tumbled and drifted into a hundred shades of bluish gray as they crossed the sun. Jake got lost in them and jumped at the touch of a hand on his shoulder.

Amanda signed apologetically. *I'm sorry.*

I'm deaf. Don't sneak up on me.

He pointed at the spot next to him until Amanda sat down hesitantly. The trouble with lip reading was that he had to look right at Amanda. He had to search her face and watch her mouth, and there weren't enough calluses on his heart to do it painlessly.

Dead bird, she signed.

Jake nodded. What did she expect? *Stupid idea. King was right.*

"No it wasn't!" She slid right around in front of him and glared. Her blue eyes were full of pain and frustration. "I can't do anything right on this island,

159

not the way you can. I knew you'd make fun of me, I knew you'd laugh at me, Jake, but I tried."

Stupid idea. Not laughing.

"Well, I failed. I failed all week. The bird's dead, as dead as my relationship with Chris."

Jake frowned, sure he'd misread her lips. *Say again.*

Amanda turned her face away but Jake could already see she was fighting for composure. The ring was still on her finger; he must have misunderstood. He waited — for what seemed forever — till she looked back up at him.

King? He dared to ask.

Amanda stared hard at the sky and sucked at her lips. "All week I kept waiting. I don't even know what for . . . something, something to feel right again. I thought it was the island. I thought I could make him love the island the way I do now."

Love the island? You?

Me. "I thought he might care, even pretend to care about this place for me, because it was important to me. It wasn't just the island, it was everything."

Jake caught every word. Couldn't she see that he knew those feelings? Didn't she see how close to his heart those feelings were? *This place isn't for King*, he signed.

Amanda seemed to laugh and then choke on her words. "No, I guess not. Poor dead bird." She pressed her hand over her eyes and Jake looked away.

Over where she'd buried the seagull, the birds had settled back down, and the turbulent weather made the trees sway. The hot wind felt good on his bare skin. From behind the clouds, rays from the

160

hidden sun darted right down into the bay. Jake forgot himself and turned around to see if Amanda had noticed.

When she looked from the sky to him, Jake circled his face and closed his fingers: *Beautiful*.

She nodded and tried to smile. *Beautiful*. "Why couldn't Chris . . ."

Jake had no desire to ask what she meant. Memory grabbed him. He didn't want to think about how wonderful she'd made him feel the last time she'd cried. Back then he'd been a hero, until she'd learned the truth. The week had changed Jake. His eyes were colder, he was distant. He didn't dare recall any of the Fourth of July because he didn't trust his heart and he didn't trust hers.

Chapter 20

Amanda was determined to hold on to what was left of her composure. She'd had enough of boys to last a lifetime. No more tears in front of Jake, no more pouring her heart out. Her life was a disaster.

Jake had signed, but he hadn't spoken a word to her in over a week. They both knew why, and she wasn't sure she could blame him. She knew she should say something about the laundromat, but she was afraid to bring it up. She could practically tell by looking at him that he'd kept it all locked inside, just as she had. What if he got furious again?

He signed, *Good-bye.*

Amanda took a deep breath and bent her fingers. *Friends?*

Jake looked back at the clouds and shrugged. *Yes.*

They parted and she started for Pilgrim House. Maybe she could work her way back and salvage some of their friendship. Maybe she could figure out what had happened with Chris.

For the third night, thunder rumbled in the humid night air and fog lay thick over the bay. The foghorn at the lighthouse kept Amanda awake and she spent hours in the dark fighting her unhappiness. Why didn't it just rain and get it over with? Why didn't she just cry? She was filled to bursting, just like the clouds.

It was eighty degrees at dawn. The pretty clouds were gone and the fog burned off to a hazy glare by breakfast. Because Chris had had no interest in exploring "Pilgrim stuff," the Aldens had put off their day trip to Plymouth until he left. Amanda put on the kind of makeup she'd worn in Lockwood and a dressy piqué sundress. She left Chris's ring on the bureau.

Downstairs, while they ate, she listened to Eric and Todd talk about the picnic and found herself dreading it. Her father started in on the historic accuracy of colonial life the guides portrayed at Plimoth Plantation, and Amanda thought about Chris. When her stepmother opened a brochure for the *Mayflower*, Amanda stood up.

All of it closed in on her. Her life was a shambles and she had to set it right. "I can't go," she blurted out.

Conversation stopped. "Excuse me?" Dr. Alden replied.

163

"I can't leave. I have to stay here. You have to go without me."

"Amanda, don't be silly. We won't be back until after dinner."

Amanda looked at her stepmother. "I'm not silly now! I've been silly all week, all summer. I've made a mess of everything." The hated tears sprang back. "I need to figure things out. I don't know what's wrong with me." Her feelings were so spontaneous that she didn't know what to say next.

Her stepmother got up from her chair. "I'll tell Sharon Hackett you'll be here alone. As long as there's an adult you can turn to in an emergency, I'll feel better letting you stay. I know the Hacketts have a CB or something."

Dr. Alden looked astonished but his wife shook her finger at him.

"Do you mean it?" Amanda asked.

Her stepmother hugged her and started for the screen door. "I was fifteen once, believe it or not. The rest of you get ready for our trip; I'll be back as soon as I speak with Sharon."

Jake was hilling the potato plants and draping them with protective netting when his mother came to the garden and explained Nancy Alden's sudden appearance and departure.

Amanda would be alone on the island for the day. He knew his mother wouldn't let her sit around Pilgrim House by herself. He should have gone out lobstering with his father.

His mother was all smiles as she signed to him. *Go and get her when you've finished. Bring her over here. Swim. Ride. Time together.*

Jake shook his head. *I have to take my boat out, check my traps. She'll come here by herself. You'll see.*

His mother arched her eyebrows but didn't argue, and Jake pretended to get lost in his work. He was still in the garden, pulling up the dead pea vines, when Amanda appeared.

She was way out at the edge of the pasture, where it dropped down to the shore. She stood out there looking at the water, and the sight of her riveted Jake where he stood. He'd never seen her in a dress and she dazzled him all over again. She looked wistful, and the thin, white cotton billowed around her in the hot breeze. She gathered her skirt and scrambled over the low stone wall, then brushed something from her shoulder. She seemed to float, as if she were at the surface of his drowning pool, caught in her own unhappiness. He wanted to think it served her right. She picked up a stray feather and twirled it in her fingers sadly.

Thunder hammered in Jake's chest, and the prickly feelings he wouldn't name danced through him. He ached to go closer but couldn't bare to hear more talk of Chris. Those problems were Amanda's, and her heartache didn't begin to touch his.

Jake turned around and carried the vines to the compost pile, willing himself to concentrate on dead peas and longing for the lobster boat under his feet. It was time to check his traps.

His mother knew his plans and it saved him. As Amanda wandered down to his house, Jake waited, then crossed the meadow and went down to the boathouse and his pier.

The unsettled weather and turbulent skies produced swells across the bay. They came in from open sea and were barely noticeable at the island, but around the point of the Gurnet, breakers crashed the beaches. Stephen Hackett had gone out at dawn, not very optimistic about finding calm seas. The waves that packed the beaches with body surfers and skimboarders was the bane of those in working boats.

Jake worked from his father's fifteen-foot motorboat, *Runaway*. Equipped with a small outboard engine and VHF marine radio, it was big enough to get him out to the traps he set himself and perfect for skimming around the bay.

He filled the engine with gasoline and put the can back in the boathouse, pulled his heavy rubber work boots over his jeans, and carried the bait bucket out to the pier. Amanda was on the beach when he came back out. She watched him, but there was no reaction to the pungent fish remains he carried.

To Jake, the contrast seemed absurd. She stood against the breeze, and her melancholy expression pulled at him like a magnet. A strap slid from her shoulder, the feather in her fingers was a gull's. He was close enough to see that it was a mottled brown as she began to sign.

Hello, Jake.

He put down the bucket. *Hello, Mayflower.*

No father work today.

Jake knew what she meant and shook his head as he continued down the pier to his boat. Obviously she'd only walked through the pasture because she'd thought he was out at sea and she wouldn't run into him. He looked at the bay, but even for Jake the silence dragged. Once again she walked up behind him and tapped him on the shoulder, making him jump.

"Your mother said you'd take me in the boat."

He looked her up and down and shook his head.

Amanda got the message. "I'll change. Give me a minute."

No way! No! Sorry! Rough weather. No boat.

"Please, Jake, I need to talk to you." She ran her index finger back and forth at her lips. *Talk. You and me.* She curved her fingers to form the letter *C*: *communicate.* "Your mother knows where I am. She says we're to come in if the clouds get serious. *Understand?*"

Of course I understand. Yes.

"You're making this very tough! Help me, I'm not a mind reader."

That's a relief.

She looked confused.

He shrugged. Why didn't she give up?

"Don't leave without me." With that, Amanda turned and disappeared up the path.

He should have left. He should have gone out alone where there was nothing but sky and water and backbreaking work to keep him from thinking, but he didn't. He waited, and Amanda came back in jeans and a shirt, as if she planned to lend a hand.

Reluctantly, he helped her into the boat and felt confident enough to smile as her expression changed. The boat reeked of the work, like the *Sharon* and the back of the fish market, and Jake thought of the rolling sea. Had she considered the fact that she might be seasick the entire time?

She stayed quietly beside him as he skimmed past

the island. As they puttered their way out along the barrier spit, Amanda looked at the buoys. *Yours?*

No. Out further.

From the salt marsh where they'd run aground, to the crowds on the public beach, Jake looked at Amanda's two worlds. He began to relax in spite of himself. He was in control. He knew his boat and the bay, and despite everything, Amanda's closeness charged him with energy.

Jake pointed to a cloud formation and signed, *Beautiful.*

"Chris never looked," she replied. "Never cared."

He turned back from watching her speak and took his hands from the throttle. *You love him.*

Amanda lifted her left hand. She tapped her empty ring finger. "No more ring. I don't know anything about love. *Nothing about love.*"

Sorry. It was the only reply Jake could think of. Amanda looked pained as she read his face.

They traveled in silence into the open waters between the Gurnet and Plymouth's shores. They moved against the incoming tide, riding the small swells up and down. Amanda looked pale.

Jake grabbed his stomach and stuck out his tongue.

Amanda laughed and nodded. "A little bit seasick, yes."

The boat rocked gently. Jake set the engine at idle and pointed to a floating buoy. *Mine.*

With his rubber gloves on, he pulled hard and hauled the trap up from where it lay, twenty feet below. Amanda balanced the weight of the trap by staying opposite it, and he caught the whiff of her cologne again, like the sweatshirt. Risk.

He laughed at her surprise when she realized how heavy the trap was, and her excitement when the trap held a "keeper," a lobster of regulation size. He pulled it from the interior net, banded the powerful claws, and stuffed the flounder remains into the bait pocket.

More traps.

He maneuvered his boat to the next one and the next. There were only a few set out in this spot. They weren't the hundreds or the attached trawls he and his father set, but they were his. There was a crab in the second, which he threw back, and a lobster in the third.

As usual, it was messy work, and Jake was aware of the effort Amanda was making. She wasn't squeamish. She complimented him as he banded the claws and barely grimaced when kelp and sea bottom slid down her leg from the trap.

Jake stuffed flounder remains into the small circular net of the next trap and lowered it back into the water. *I'm sorry about your bird.*

Say again, she signed.

Dead bird. Sorry.

Stupid.

Since they had no choice but to look closely at each other, something lifted in both of them. In Amanda, the wariness was replaced by sadness, as deep as the day before.

Jake looked at her and signed. *Island not for King.*

"It was more than the island. There were lots of things I'd never noticed before. I was so busy wanting to love him that I didn't notice the way he really is. It's not his fault. It's as if the Chris King in my head is a totally different person from the real one."

Mayflower, it hurts when someone isn't what you want them to be.

Say again, Jake.

He raised his hands but Amanda grabbed them. "Please, I want to know what you're saying. Speak, too. I don't know enough sign yet. Tell me what you're signing."

Something locked tight in his chest. He couldn't.

Chapter
21

"Jake, you haven't spoken to me since the laundromat."

He clenched his jaw.

Amanda let go of his hands and gripped his shoulders. "I know why. I know how angry and hurt you were. I did the wrong thing, but I wanted to help."

The rocking of the boat made her hold onto the coaming. "I'm so sorry it happened, but it did. I need your help, Jake. I care about what you think. I want to know everything you tell me. Your voice is funny but I understand."

He fooled with a rubber claw band, then put it down. "It hurts — *hurts* — *when you make up people in your head. When they don't love what you*

171

love." Jake stopped. He'd said too much, revealed too much.

Amanda turned, and he wasn't surprised to see her press her hands over her eyes. He knew her gestures and the way she fought tears. Jake had no experience with this, only gut feelings, and even those he hardly dared to trust. Instinct told him to wait.

Her eyes were damp but she was smiling as she signed as much as she could and then spoke. "*You're deaf, Jake*, but you listen better than people with ears that work. You know about things that matter, about people's hearts. I guess mine is broken."

He didn't dare think about his own.

After a week with Chris's shallowness, Amanda was overwhelmed with Jake's insight. She'd shut him out for more than a week and taken his friendship for granted. No wonder he was keeping her at arm's length. Jake was like a book, and if Amanda were to get to know him, it would have to be one page at a time. She couldn't hurry him; she'd done enough damage already.

Jake shifted and rubbed his neck. A sudden swell beneath the boat made it rock precariously and they grabbed the coaming. The concern in Jake's expression made Amanda follow his gaze as he scanned the sky. It was still pearl gray and the glare off the water made Amanda squint.

Concern fluttered in her, too, as she tapped Jake's shoulder. "How many more traps to check?"

He held up six fingers.

A gust broke the steady breeze and slapped Amanda's hair against the side of her face. She looked across the empty stretch of water. Out beyond them the sea swells that the little boat had been riding began to break into small peaks, and when the next gust blew, whitecaps flew with them.

As sea spray covered them, Jake handed Amanda a life jacket from under the forward seat and put on his own. "Jake, this is getting rough!"

He nodded without commenting and headed the boat in the direction of the next pot, farther off shore.

Amanda thought of the line squall that had caught her in the meadow weeks earlier and her heart hammered. They came up from nowhere, that much she knew. She looked again for thunderheads, but the sky hadn't changed. At least she thought it hadn't. The distant Plymouth skyline had dissolved into the glare.

Jake shielded his eyes with his hand, shook his head, and reached for the handle of the outboard motor. He should never have sat there talking, thinking only about her old boyfriends and love. He should have watched the sky every minute.

Home? Amanda asked.

Jake nodded. "Work with me. Two traps on the way. Too rough for more, maybe rain."

She didn't like the sound of any of it. "Home, the sooner the better. Tell me what to do."

Jake pointed at the next floating buoy as the rough water jostled it. A swell followed the boat, lifting it forward as the buoy rose. Amanda's stomach mimicked the motion and she felt as though she'd been pumped with air. The smell of bait and sea bottom was stronger than ever.

Jake slapped her on the back of her life preserver.

"Breathe the air, away from the smell." Amanda nodded, thinking she must look absolutely green.

Another gust whipped across the swells, splattering her and making her shiver. She was surprised at how chilly she was. She didn't have the sealegs that Jake did, and it was becoming more and more of an effort to keep her balance.

The next swell shook the boat and threw them both off balance. Amanda slid against Jake and knocked his arm. He grabbed her but not before the boat veered into the buoy. With a grinding *thud* the boat stopped and strained against the waves.

"Prop! The trap line fouled the prop," Jake cried. He turned off the engine and tried to raise it so the blades came out of the water.

Amanda felt as though they were in some crazy tug of war — and losing. The lobster pot below the surface tugged at them and held them in place while the swells of the incoming tide pushed at the stern as they headed toward shore.

Spray hit Jake's shoulder. "Forward!"

Amanda shook her head. *Say again*, she tried.

Jake pointed to the bow.

Amanda fought panic as she looked at Jake's concerned expression. The air in her stomach had been replaced with fear. She felt totally helpless, without enough knowledge or strength. She tripped over the lobster bin but scrambled as far forward as she could. From there she eyed the VHF and reminded herself that help was a call away. If Jake couldn't free the line, she'd call Mack Howland. Maybe the *Sharon* was right there, too, someplace close, just caught in the haze.

Once Amanda's weight was distributed forward,

Jake worked frantically at the line but it held tight. The sea lifted the boat at the back, as if giant hands were pushing it up to look for something under the stern. Even up front, Amanda could feel the pressure on the back as the line held them taut.

The colors above her were changing. It was growing grayer and colder, much colder. She'd had enough science to know that a sweeping cold front on a blistering day could produce violent changes in the weather.

Jake signaled again, this time for her to come astern. Their best hope was raising the pot. They should have been well on their way to the island by now. In the shelter of the barrier beach the storm wouldn't do more than soak them. Amanda put out her hand to steady herself and Jake took it, guiding her gingerly toward himself so that she wouldn't displace too much weight.

It would have worked perfectly except a third gust hit them dead astern. Instead of lifting the boat, the swell smashed across the engine, the sternboard, and Jake before it filled the bottom.

"Water's in the boat," Amanda cried.

Jake's face was ghostly white.

"Jake — "

He put his hands on either side of her face. "Help me. *You and me*. Don't panic. Okay?"

Amanda tried to nod but thunder cracked, louder than the sea and the pounding of her heart, and she crumpled into the cockpit of the boat.

Chapter
22

Jake signed, *Thunder?*
Yes!

Water sloshed over the lobster bin as Jake went back to the stern. Every muscle in his arms strained as he worked to lift the trap with what line he could reach.

They needed help and they needed it now. Amanda tried to think as rationally as she could. Then it seemed so apparent. She reached for the hand-held mike of the marine radio. If the *Sharon* were out, it would be closer to them than the harbormaster. With the wind in her face, she pushed down the button with her thumb and spoke as clearly as she could. "*Runaway* calling the *Sharon*," she said twice. Please answer, she prayed.

The VHF was silent, not even the crackle of dead air.

Amanda squeezed harder. "*Sharon*, please answer." It was then that she realized she'd kept the button pressed and wouldn't have heard a reply. She released her thumb to immediate crackling, but no answer.

The gusts had settled into continuous blasts of driving wind, fed by the hot, humid air and the cold sea. The front that had played over the Atlantic all week was finally serious. Visibility diminished further until the Gurnet Light was no longer in sight. They bobbed and rolled like a Hackett buoy as Amanda tried again to get help.

"Caterham harbormaster, Caterham harbormaster, this is *Runaway*." Jake fell backward into the ankle-deep saltwater. "Mayday!" This time she let go of the button.

"*Runaway*, this is the Caterham harbormaster. Switch and answer channel twelve."

Amanda twirled the dial on the radio and pressed the button down as she began to choke out the information.

Mack Howland's voice was calm but urgent. "State your location, *Runaway*."

"I don't know!"

Jake's biggest fear had been Amanda. Her seasickness and panicky expression as they got into trouble worried him as much as the fouled line. Though he couldn't read her lips from where he was, it calmed him to see her speaking into the radio. He'd been fighting dependency and help-lessness all his life, and even as she helped, he hated depending on her voice.

"Where are we? Where are we?"

Jake stared at her. "Bennett's Ledge, off Gurnet Light."

"Say again." *Say again, Jake!* she signed desperately.

Wasting precious minutes, Jake finger spelled as she repeated it. The minute he'd finished she nodded wildly and kissed him hard. She was so desperate, she turned to the mike and repeated the letters to Mack Howland. "B E N N E T T S L E D G E. Bennett's Ledge, that's it! Off Gurnet Light!"

Jake forced himself to think. His hands were raw from the line, and the saltwater stung as it washed the trickles of blood across his knuckles and over his palm. Cutting the line and freeing the boat from the trap would set them adrift. Did Amanda realize they were sinking? It was just a matter of time, and he was forced to decide which course would keep them afloat longer.

The first ballast to go was the bin of lobsters. Without a second glance, he maneuvered it up onto the coaming and dumped it over. Amanda grabbed him then and looked at his face. The taste of salt-water in his mouth was the only clue that the driving wet was sea, not rain. The wind tore at Jake's ears and roared in Amanda's, and when the water reached shin level, he reached for his jackknife. The line dug into his already tender hands as he sliced and hacked it in half. The moment the boat was

178

free, the stern rose and rolled as the lobster trap sank back to the sea bottom forever.

With nothing to hold them, the rocking grew ominous and the gathering storm tossed the boat. Amanda tried to bail with her hands. Jake scanned the sky. Experience and knowledge made him expect the worst. He moved back to Amanda. "Tell me, thunder."

The fright deepened in her eyes, but she nodded. "Help is coming. How long from Caterham?"

Jake didn't smile. "Too long."

Never! You and I, Jake, together. Okay. Help is coming. The boat heeled to the side and water slapped her face. The starboard side disappeared as she screamed and scrambled. Jake caught her by her life jacket and hauled her with him to the other side, but the minute the boat righted itself, he pushed her back to balance them.

She stayed where she was and bailed what she could as Jake continued to cut away the line in the propeller blade. It wasn't until she looked at the blood stains on her soaking life jacket that she realized he was bleeding.

It never occurred to Jake that he might die. His fear was of losing Amanda. If they went over, would she stay with the boat? Did she know how to swim well? Why hadn't he asked her! There wasn't time now. A swell broke over the engine and the stern dipped below the water.

Fresh water pelted them as the skies let go. With a sickening tilt, first to port and then to starboard, the boat filled. Jake pulled hard at his boots as water poured into them, weighing him down like an anchor.

He'd gotten his first boot off when the full force of the line squall hit. Eighty-mile-an-hour winds sliced the words from him as he yelled, "Stay with the boat, stay with the boat," not knowing that the roar of the storm smothered his words.

The pelting rain forced him to close his eyes and reduced the visibility to inches. The boat seemed to shrink as the ocean tossed around them. Suddenly the sea rose up again, gathered itself around them, and rolled into the boat.

With one boot still on, Jake reached for Amanda and she grabbed his life jacket. The boat filled completely and heaved under the brunt of the storm. As the two of them hit the water, he pushed her away and disappeared under the swells, desperate to remove the boot that filled with water and tugged like a cement block around his ankle.

"Jake!" Amanda tried to clear her brain. The life jacket would keep him afloat. They had to stay with the boat. The swells disoriented her and she had no idea where shore was. Over and over she told herself that Jake knew what to do. If he didn't die, if he didn't leave her, and she could just follow his lead, they'd survive. He couldn't die, not Jake. She loved him.

He'd have to hang on, too; help was on the way.

"Jake!" She took a mouthful of water and choked. The next swell pulled at her as she reached for the hull of the boat. It was slippery, but she managed to inch her way along the side to the stern, where she could hold onto the fouled propellor. As she reached it, a hand grabbed her wrist.

Jake appeared beside her, but as she threw her arms around his neck, he pushed away again and locked his hands around her waist. As the storm beat down on them, he pushed her and indicated that she slide up onto the hull. Once she was on, he worked his way to the other side and came up facing her. Once again, he locked his hands around her wrists and she did the same as they kept each other from drowning.

The storm had come up in fifteen minutes and in another fifteen, the squall slid over them and hit the island. The roaring in Amanda's ears lessened and, although the swells continued, without the wind the rain became a downpour.

Her fingers ached and pain shot through her shoulders as the sea pulled her and she gripped Jake. The cold ocean was numbing her, but she fought all of it and refused to let go of him as they lay across the boat hull. Every few seconds Jake squeezed her wrists in two short jabs and she'd answer by squeezing his. It was the only communication left to them as they waited.

Chapter
23

Amanda heard the boat before she saw it. The low roar of the harbormaster's inboard engine seemed to fill her, coming right through the water, and the hull, into her bones. She looked at the swells rising around her in time to catch sight of it as it appeared behind Jake.

The rest was a blur of motion and yellow foul-weather gear. Mack Howland hauled her up, and before she could think, he sat her down and wrapped her in a blanket, life jacket and all. There was somebody else hugging her — Jake's father. He leaned over and brought his son aboard, tucking the rough woolen army blanket around his shoulders.

Mack Howland went back to the wheel and talked into the VHF. Then both men worked frantically to secure the submerged motorboat to the stern of the harbormaster's boat. The trip to shore was long and arduous and Amanda couldn't imagine that Mack knew where he was going. She sat huddled in silence as they cut through the slapping water. Finally there was more commotion and idling of engines as the bumpers dangling over the sides took the brunt of their arrival at the Hackett pier.

More yellow blur — Mrs. Hackett in her slicker putting out her hand. Amanda's knees wobbled as she tried to stand up but Jake caught her. He unbuckled her life jacket and peeled off his own. Then, with one arm around her waist and one holding the soaking blanket over them, he started with her through the storm and up the bluff to the farm. He was so close she could feel how badly he was shaking from the cold, or maybe she was shaking. It was hard to hurry, but they had to.

Once in the kitchen, Mrs. Hackett took the blanket and moved them along to the bathroom. Amanda tried to concentrate as Mrs. Hackett explained that the storm would keep her parents overnight in Plymouth and that she was to stay where she was. Her family was safe. "And so are you," Mrs. Hackett added, giving her a hug. "You two need all the hot water we've got," she said as she turned on the shower.

"Get right in there, clothes and all. Jake knows just what to do. Be thankful it's summer. We'd have lost you for sure to the cold alone. I'll have tea when you're through."

Without a word, Jake nudged her into the tub and

followed. He turned on the shower, which seemed to Amanda no warmer than the sea had been. Her shaking stayed violent and she tried to adjust the dial.

Under the pelting water, Jake shook his head. *Let me. Cold first.*

Gradually he adjusted the dial, bringing heated water down on them, insuring that their body temperatures stayed normal. Even the soaking-wet denim and cotton helped press the warmth into them. Amanda gave herself the luxury of letting somebody else take over. From the very beginning, Jake had known what to do. She had been in Jake's world. Trusting him had saved her on the boat and he was saving her now.

All the fight had gone out of Amanda. Jake stayed in the shower till the hot water ran out. He ached to hold her and apologize for everything, as if he had some control over the forces in their universe.

Instead he kept his hands on the shower controls, and when the hot water finally ran out, he turned it off, took his towel, and went into his room to change. His father joined him and talked of salvaging the boat, reassuring him that insurance would pay for it if it were a total loss. He complimented his son on his coolheadedness while he bandaged his hands and listened as Jake relived the nightmare.

The kitchen was empty, but it smelled of biscuits and chicken. The teapot was under the cozy and two mugs sat waiting. Jake took a carrot and pulled his slicker from its peg. The storm had settled down to a light, steady rain, although the evening sky still flashed with distant lightning. He had to keep moving so that he didn't think about what could have happened.

Once in the barn, he hung the slicker on the tack wall. His horse was in her stall. Jake took a brush and began the long, even strokes along her hide that helped him clear his head. He wasn't shaking anymore — the shower had chased the cold — but inside him there was a numbness the warm water couldn't reach. He turned to fill Lightning's feed bin, and the numbness spread up into his heart.

Amanda was standing against the tack wall. There was no ray of sunlight this time, no halo bathing her wet hair. The dark gold strands curled against her cheek and droplets of water puddled all over the shoulders of her borrowed rain gear. She hung the raincoat next to his, and he saw that besides a pair of his mother's shorts, she was wearing his sweatshirt.

"I came to get you for dinner." She circled her heart. *I'm sorry about your boat. Are you okay?*

Yes.

But sad?

Sad was much too simple a word for the layers of emotion strangling him. *Yes, sad. I'm sorry, too.*

"I fell against you. I knocked your arm. It's my fault we ran over the line."

Weather.

"Jake — "

He was swimming again, through the drowning pool, but this time he put out his hand to her. *Thank you, Mayflower. You saved my life.*

Amanda looked confused.

He added words to his signs this time. *"You saved my life."*

185

She signed what she knew. *"Me? You! You saved us, Jake. You told me what to do, you did everything. If you hadn't been there, I would have drowned!"*

"I'm deaf. You called the harbormaster."

Amanda tapped his chest. "Jake Hackett, just because my ears work, do you think I'd have lasted five minutes out there without you?" She laughed as if relief were pushing the happiness through her. "Oh, Jake, we saved *each other*. Maybe we survived because you and I trusted each other. Is it so terrible that you needed me? I sure needed you."

Amanda hoped she looked more confident than she felt. At fifteen, it was a terrifying feeling to realize her life had been in Jake's hands. She wanted to understand his silence, to feel what he felt. She went back to square one and bent her fingers. *Friends. "Friends trust each other, Jake. I love your world, and friends can love each other."*

Something pushed away Jake's numbness, a feeling that left him warm, hardly daring to believe what she was telling him. Amanda Alden made him feel whole. She made him angry and frustrated, she made him think, she made him laugh. She made him search himself, and best of all, she made him feel very, very much alive. He finally understood that none of it would come without trusting her, and all of it, even the bad stuff, was worth the risk.

Jake opened his arms. Amanda snuggled into his hug and their hearts hammered against each other. In the barn full of the island smells, of horse and lobster traps and the green freshness of the rain, they stood that way for a long time and then Amanda looked up at him. Her blue eyes sparkled. "Will you ever kiss me again?"

With his arms around her, Jake felt too good to let go. "Now," he said as clearly as he could, "and for the rest of the summer."

Amanda put her own hands up. *Friends, Jake. You and me forever.*

Chapter
24

They didn't have forever; what they had was the rest of the summer. Jake didn't like thinking about it, but reality crept in around every other thought in his head. At the end of the month, Amanda would be gone. Maybe not back to Christopher King, but back to her other life, her real life.

That night she slept in his sister's empty room. Jake stood outside her closed door for a long time when he rose in the morning. He had another life, too — high school, mainland people — but it never felt real the way the island did.

It wasn't much past dawn, but the empty kitchen smelled of coffee. He walked outside, where drizzle hung in the still air. The sea was calm again, the prevailing winds not yet up, and the pier was empty. His father had already taken the *Sharon* into the Caterham marina, where Mack Howland had towed the motorboat.

When Jake went back into the house, his mother and Amanda were at the kitchen table. He sat and watched them talk about the accident. Amanda didn't seem any the worse for having nearly drowned; in fact, she looked excited and as happy as he'd ever seen her. It was then, over pancakes and maple syrup, that Jake resolved to make the most of what time they had left.

The Aldens returned to the island on the afternoon tide and heard the details of the accident from Jake's parents, who added lots of reassurance to their descriptions. Todd and Eric thought the whole thing sounded awesome.

During August, Jake went out on the *Sharon* when he was needed, but it still left time for Amanda. Often she'd meet the lobster boat, and Jake's heart would race as they came round the island and he'd spot her in silhouette on the bluff.

If it was hot, they'd swim, and in the cool of the day they'd hike to all the places Amanda had once hated. He kissed her under the pines and out in the cemetery and wished, for the thousandth time, that it would last forever.

When they got back into a boat together, it was at Amanda's invitation to sail. Instead of lobstering, Jake met her at Pilgrim House and carried lunch while she toted a canvas bag of towels. The dog days of August were muggy, and the wind felt wonderful as they skimmed around the marshes off the barrier beach.

Amanda pointed to the estuary, where they'd run aground weeks before. "Take me back there."

Jake shrugged. "Periwinkles and mud flats?" *Mud flats?*

Yes.

Careful to avoid the delicate eel grass, Jake maneuvered the little boat as close to shore as possible. When they were completely aground, the two of them got out and tugged it onto what little beach there was.

Amanda stood on the sand with the breeze in her hair and looked across to the island. Sometimes it felt as though she were a different person from the one dragged from home last June, a person she liked much better. She caught Jake watching her and she grinned at him, knowing it would make him blush. *Wind, Jake of the Island.*

He nodded. *Tell me how the wind sounds.*

Amanda stepped close to him.

At first she shrugged, but then she closed her eyes and put her face into the breeze. After a moment she turned and with a half smile, she blew on his cheek.

He nodded shyly.

Amanda put her arms around his neck. "I'm going to take all this home with me, Jake. All this is part of me now. You made it part of me."

"Memories."

She put her arms down and nodded. *Good ones.* "Don't be too sad or I'll fall apart."

You?

Me.

190

Other life, Mayflower. "You have another life."

Amanda looked out at the lapping shoreline before she made eye contact again so that he could read her lips. "I do, Jake. You do, too."

He shook his head.

Yes. "School, friends, girls in Caterham."

"Not like you."

"I don't have boys in Lockwood like you. No one else is like you."

Deaf. Jake tapped his ear and started to bring his hands together but she swatted them apart before he finished the sign.

"It isn't that you're deaf. It's that you're special."

Jake turned and began to walk along the edge of the eel grass until Amanda dogged him. When she caught up, she grabbed his arm and stood in front of him. "Same old trick. Walk away from what's on your mind. Talk to me!"

Talk to her! How could he tell her that she'd opened a door, only to have the end of summer slam it shut? How could he explain that his "other" life was just getting by till spring came around again? How could Amanda understand that when she left it would be worse than if she'd never come at all?

Still facing him, she tried her best to smile. "You think everything's over." *Finished.* "You think we can't write? We can't visit?"

"Not the same. We can't even talk on the phone."

"A visit, Jake. You might have to come into *my* world. You might have to wear shoes and shake hands. Maybe go to a dance."

Even kidding him couldn't keep the tears down. Though she blinked them away, her throat got tight, making her grateful that Jake couldn't hear the catch in her voice. "When I go back to Lockwood, my world will be different because I'll be different. Your specialness made me — I don't know — whole. It'll be like you're with me, even when you're not, because I'll see things the way you do."

Thank you, Mayflower, was all he could manage.

Amanda smiled again. "I can do that for you, too, Jake. In your other life, in your school, I can make you more like the others. It's happening already. You can think of me, too. You can remember us and how it is to talk with a girl, how it can be easier than you think." She tapped his shoulder. "You can make me jealous this winter."

Jake pulled her roughly to him and kissed her. Why would he ever want somebody else? Who would there be who could get into his head the way Mayflower did?

Amanda sighed against him and wiped her eyes by pulling Jake's shirt to her face. When she felt better, she walked with him back to the boat and pulled out the canvas bag. Under the towels she'd brought her boom box. Without another word, she set it on the dry sand, found a station she liked, and opened her arms to Jake.

He stood rooted to the beach, so she danced alone at first, turning slowly in her pink sundress. Her gestures were exaggerated, which made it easy for him to pick up the beat. One-and-two-and-three-and-four-and . . . no different from his music classes all through school.

Amanda wiggled. "I planned to get you to dance with me and I figured it was safe here. Dancing can be your key. It's going to unlock some of those doors, Jake."

He furrowed his brow.

"Dancing will make you more like everybody else." She pointed to his foot. "I saw you, Jake Hackett! I saw you tap that toe. Now come on . . ." She ran to him and, once again, went into his arms. She got him into position and then, on the hard sand so they wouldn't shift, she began to lead.

It was a slow song, a foxtrot with the one, two, three, four beat. Jake was stiff and self-conscious, so Amanda melted all the more. She was loose and romantic until the song changed, then flip and outrageous, and she wouldn't let up until Jake tried it all, too. They ended the afternoon in laughter because it felt better than tears.

Amanda saved her last request until their final week together. He wanted to take her into Caterham and she insisted on a "real" date. She got the use of the Alden Whaler and Jake got the keys to the truck, still parked at the landing.

They left the island at dusk, Jake in khakis and a lightweight sweater, Amanda in a dress.

On the way across the channel, Amanda asked about the motorboat still being repaired, and Jake offered to show it to her when they reached the landing. Her plans for their date had been set off by a simple poster she'd spotted in the post office.

They docked the boat and walked to the neighboring marina. Amanda could hear the band from the street, though Jake had no idea of what was happening until they entered the yard. Part of the parking lot was roped off and marked with helium balloons. A rock band, in full swing, was playing from risers and hundreds of Caterham teenagers were dancing and milling around the barrels of soft drinks and tables of food.

Jake's expressive face told Amanda everything she needed to know. He was unpleasantly surprised at her trick; he should have known she'd be up to something, and he had no intention of staying.

She grabbed his arm as if they were about to be separated. *One dance.*

No way.

Coward. Turkey.

He laughed in spite of himself. *You mean chicken.* "Not if you'll dance with me."

They stood together long enough for friends to recognize him, and at Amanda's insistence, she was introduced. From there, she took over. Before the set ended, she'd managed to get the two of them involved with what she assumed were his friends from school.

A boy named Matt asked her to dance, and she turned her back on Jake so he couldn't read her lips. "I want to dance with Jake."

Matt laughed. "No way. He'll go to these things once in a while, but that's it. He never dances."

Amanda turned around and looked at Jake. "Do you want me to dance with Matt or will you come out there with me?"

Jake's pounding heart sank, and he hated Amanda for cornering him. He didn't reply.

"We're wasting a good song. Make up your mind."

Deaf. Can't hear it.

"Sorry, Jake, that's no excuse. *I can hear it.*" She tugged his wrist as the others drifted back on the floor.

"Your world, Amanda, not mine."

194

"This is your world, too. This is your town, and these guys could be your friends. Holy cow, Jake, you can't be scared of music when you tackle the ocean, for heaven's sake!"

Say again.

Dance with me.

There was no fight left in him. He ached to dance with her. The clock ticking away the little time they had left made him just desperate enough to put his arms around her. Amanda took it from there.

They didn't venture far, but they danced. The slow dances were easy, as Amanda moved against him and tapped the rhythm on his shoulder. The fast ones were tougher, but for the first time, Jake realized a lot of the guys were as bad as he was!

They stayed for the rest of the night, sometimes dancing, sometimes joining in conversation. Toward the end of the night, Matt tried again. "Once?"

Amanda looked at Jake. "Sure."

Jake watched them walk into the crowd of dancers and hated everything he felt. A girl named Jennifer, who'd shared his English class, had been standing with the group. It wasn't until she put down her soda that he realized she was talking to him.

"Dance, Jake?"

He looked at the crowd: slow dance. Jennifer moved into his arms. She felt entirely different from Amanda. He stepped on her foot and felt the heat on his cheeks, but she was laughing and shaking her head. It didn't seem to matter, and when he finally relaxed, he wasn't too awkward.

Amanda and Jake stayed till the end and took the boat back to the island at midnight. The moon was bright, and the beam cast from the running lights splintered on the water as they moved in the darkness. Amanda held the big marine light and Jake docked the boat at Pilgrim House. Teamwork made the going easier in the dark, and they were quiet until he'd walked her up to the kitchen. Jake stood for a long time and looked at her in the yellow gaslight coming through the window.

Thank you, Mayflower.

"Your world, Jake. Nice." A sharp stab of jealousy made her heart ache. Jake would go on, just as she would. It's what had to be; it was what he needed.

"I love you, Mayflower."

She couldn't speak. *I love you, too,* she signed. Enough to want everything good for you, she wanted to add. Enough to want you to be happy in all the places that make up your world, not just the space that keeps you safe.

"Will you come back?" he asked.

She nodded. *Next summer,* she signed. *Maybe before.* She wondered already what Jake's winter would bring. Amanda didn't know any more about this kind of love than Jake did. They were on equal footing, having given the best of themselves to each other. Maybe this kind of love survived. They had the time to find out.

Jake bent his head and Amanda thought he would kiss her. Instead, in the moonlight, he pulled her gently onto the grass. He tapped her shoulder — one, two, three, four — and the two of them, to no music at all, danced slowly under the fat August moon.

About the Author

LESLIE DAVIS GUCCIONE studied art for two years with Carolyn Wyeth and is a graduate of Wilmington Friends School, Wilmington, Delaware, and Queens College, Charlotte, North Carolina. She is the author of *Nobody Listens to Me* and also writes young adult and adult novels under the name Leslie Davis. Ms. Guccione lives with her husband and children in the National Historic Sea Captains' District in Duxbury, Massachusetts.

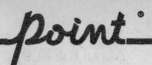

Other books you will enjoy,
about real kids like you!